# WEIGHTY MATTERS

## LINDA P. KOZAR

### AN UNTIL THE FAT LADIES SING MYSTERY

# BOOKS BY LINDA P. KOZAR

■■■■■■■■■■■■■■■■■■■■■■■■■■

UNTIL THE FAT LADIES SING MYSTERIES

*Misfortune Cookies*
*A Tisket, A Casket*
*Dead As A Doornail*
*That Wasn't Chicken*
*Felony Fruitcake*
*Weighty Matters*
*Custard's Last Stand*

UNTIL THE FAT LADIES SING MYSTERIES
■ ■ ■ ■ ■ ■ ■ ■ ■ ■ ■ ■ ■ ■ ■ ■ ■ ■ ■
BOOK SIX

# WEIGHTY MATTERS

## LINDA P. KOZAR

Kozy Kozar Books

When a traveling circus comes to the town of Wachita, Texas bad things begin to happen under the Big Top. Super-sized sleuths, Sue Jan and Lovita take to the tents to track down a crazy clown killer, even though Lovita is fixing to give birth in just a few short weeks. And if that's not enough, a scary Sasquatch is sighted in the Wachita woods, attracting a TV news reporter, a Bigfoot investigative team and a reality show film crew. The townsfolk are shaking in their cowboy boots but Sue Jan and Lovita aren't clowning around.

Published by Linda Kozar, CreateSpace Edition

© 2016 Linda Kozar

Printed in the United States of America

All rights reserved. No part of this publication may be reproduced, stored in a retrieval system, or transmitted in any form or by any means—for example, electronic, photocopy, recording—without the prior written permission of the publisher. The only exception is brief quotations in printed reviews.

This is a work of fiction. Names, characters, incidents, and dialogues are products of the author's imagination and are not to be construed as real. Any resemblance to actual events or persons, living or dead, is entirely coincidental.

Scripture taken from the HOLY BIBLE NEW INTERNATIONAL VERSION®. Copyright 1973, 1978, 1984 Biblica. Used by permission of Zondervan. All rights reserved.

# DEDICATION

*To the girls in Ohio: Marge Kozar, my mom-in-love, to Michelle Novosel, my sister-in-love, my wonderful niece, Mackenzie Novosel, and to Jesus, my sweet Savior!*

# CHAPTER ONE

## Not My Monkeys, Not My Circus

"Did you hear?" Breathless, my best friend and business partner, Sue Jan Madson, burst through the door of the Crown of Glory Beauty Salon and Boutique. She tipped her head down, hands on her knees, panting. "Lovita, d-did you hear?" Sue Jan looked up, eyes wild with excitement.

"Hear what?" I flicked off the blow dryer, my last nerve standing on end.

Now, normally, I'm supposed to handle the boutique part of the Crown of Glory Beauty Shop and Boutique, with the pretty dresses and shoes and purses and such, but when the need arises, everyone knows I step in to do blowouts, cuts, and color. Even Homecoming and Prom Do's. And this morning, as usual, the need arose.

Sue Jan messaged that she had some sort of "errand" to do on the way to work, so I wound up doing the whole shebang for her new nitpicky client, Mrs. Barlow.

"The circus is coming to Wachita!" Sue Jan batted the air as if an invisible piñata would dispense goodies.

I sniffed, which rhymes with *miffed*, which I was. "Is it 'the' circus, or 'a' circus? There's more than one circus in the world, you know."

Sue Jan stuck her tongue out. "Don't be all uppity with your language smarts, Lovita. 'A' circus is coming to town tomorrow! It's called 'More Deck Eye's Circus and *Slideshow*, and we're going!" She reached into her purse and pulled out a small bag of boiled peanuts, cracking a few open at lightning speed.

I was about to address her use of the word "Slideshow" instead of "Sideshow" when Sue Jan's pesky client spoke up.

"A circus?" Mrs. Barlow, a sixtyish, salt-and-peppery-haired woman with a beak where a nose should have been, suddenly perked up. "What kind of circus would come to this town? The only kind of circus this 'one-hearse town' would attract is a flea circus." She swiped her nose across her sleeve.

Taken aback by the one-hearse-town comment, I was about to say something, but Sue Jan's face flushed crimson and I realized we were in trouble. She treated every negative comment about our town as a personal attack on her husband, Monroe Madson, the Mayor of Wachita. I could see the venom was fixing to pour out, so I tried to deflect the situation.

"Miz Barlow, whoop-tee-do, you're all done now! In case you're in a hurry to get somewhere, I can get you from the chair to the checkout in a flash. Wanna take a look at the back of your head real fast?" I handed her a hand mirror lickety-split, and spun her around like an astronaut-in-training.

But I saw that Sue Jan couldn't contain her anger a second longer. "Miss Barlow, just what do you mean calling Wachita a one-hearse town? And what does that mean, anyway? How many hearses does a town have to have? My husband, the Honorable Monroe Madson, is the mayor, and I'll have you know that Wachita is a great place to live. And he's a great man too—thank you very much." Hands on her hips, Sue Jan hovered over the woman.

I was so busy high-fiving Sue Jan in my mind that I almost missed the next thing she said.

"Besides that, what do you know about this town anyway? You've only been here a hot second." Sue Jan brought an index finger to her temple. "Maybe you should *think* about what you say before you say it. Lovita and I grew up here, and Wachita means the world to us."

Cornelia Barlow somehow narrowed her already beady eyes. "I've been here six miserable months so far and I'm scratching off the days like a felon in a jail cell. Back off, Crisco Kid, or I'll snatch you bald!"

Sue Jan stood still as a statue for a second. Maybe two. Then I noticed her eyes widen from marble-size to what looked to me like ping-pong-ball circumference. Not a good sign.

I knew exactly what Sue Jan was feeling. The woman had touched a nerve in both of us—the fat nerve. Sue Jan and I had grown up *and out*, and always with that awful label suspended over us. Although we'd both managed to lose weight in the last couple of years, pregnancy had thrown a curve ball to our curves. I was in my eight month with my first child, feeling big as a house—and reduced at times, not in poundage, but to a crumpled dishrag of emotions. And Sue Jan's pregnancy test was likely still resting on her bathroom sink. *Which explained the bag of peanuts in her purse. Weird cravings.* She'd called me yesterday, moments after telling Monroe they were expecting baby number three—unfortunately while he was on the treadmill. Poor guy dented the sheetrock on their bedroom wall.

"Crisco Kid, eh?" Sue Jan pushed up her sleeves.

Our other stylists, Jolene and Charla stopped their styling in midair, while the rest of the robed clients hushed to a still silence. Something bad was fixing to go down. But as long as Sue Jan didn't blurt out a "custard" word, I figured we'd be okay. FYI, Sue Jan and I call cuss words, "custard words." I'm not sure how it started, but it's sort of our thing now.

I had to do something—anything, so I grabbed the hand mirror and brought it up to the woman's face. "Ah, w-why don't you take a look, Miz Barlow? What do you think?"

She scrunched her nose at the back of her head reflection. "Ugh!" Then she spun the chair the other way, face forward.

I was all set to thank her, but the words caught in my throat when my brain caught up with my ears. "W-what?"

Now here's a helpful word of advice to everyone who sits in a client chair. Never tick off your hairdresser—especially when she's holding cutting shears. I'm ashamed to admit this, but some wicked thoughts raided through my mind before I tamped them down. Aside from that, seriously, a client could go home with a really bad haircut. The kind of haircut Stevie Wonder would give you. I'm not kidding.

The crimson in Sue Jan's cheeks faded. Her lips curled into a smile, Her cheeks began to shimmy. Like a rickety dam, her lips burst open, loosing a rush of laughter.

"You heard me," the woman repeated. "There's some stray hairs over my right ear." She pointed. The woman continued her assault. "How'd you miss those? What kind of a hairdresser are you, anyway?"

I grabbed a scissors. "Here, let me snip them."

Now anyone can tell you this about me—I, Lovita Mae Horton Taylor, am mostly an even-tempered, sweet-natured, calm-and-collected type person. I don't even have to wear extra deodorant from sweating the small stuff—*hehe*. But today was fixin' to be different.

My hand trembled with pent-up anger, but I willed my fingers to grip the scissors and steady myself. Cornelia surveyed her face in the mirror as I held my breath and made the tiny snip.

She snorted her semi-approval. "Hmmm, that's a mite better, but—"

"But what?" I asked.

"I ain't getting out of this chair till you trim my nose hairs." She brought her hands to her nose and pushed up her nostril, piggy-style. "See all them black, pointy hairs sticking out? How do you expect me to walk out of this here so-called beauty shop without snipping them off? Why, I never heard of such a thing. What kind of a joint is this?"

A collective gasp sucked the air from the room, while I gulped down the "custardly" word that popped into my mind, but kept a tight rein on what came out of my mouth. "Miz Cornelia, I don't mean you any disrespect, even though *you've* disrespected our beloved town, questioned my skills as a hairdresser and small business owner, and are now asking for a whole different kind of barber service—but the answer is no. You can pop up your nose like a piggy and leave it there all day long if you want, but I'm not touching your snout with a ten-foot pole. And that's that." I exhaled.

Her mouth fixed in an "O" shape, she stood to her feet, one hand raised. "I will never, ever, ever, forever never, set foot in this place again." She scowled and pointed at me. "You'll be sorry!"

*Promise?* That's what I wanted to say. "Well, I'm sorry you feel that way, Miz Cornelia, and I'm real sorry you weren't satisfied with the service. For future reference, you might want to try the men's barbershop down the street for all your nose hair trimming needs. Consider this cut 'n style service today 'on-the-house'."

Sue Jan chimed in, with her standard marketing slogan. "And-and thanks for visiting the Crown of Glory Beauty Salon and Boutique. *We tease to please.*"

"On-the-house?" Cornelia scrunched her jaw. "I wasn't planning on paying for this lousy cut anyway." She muttered on her way to the door. "There's much better salons in Bentley. I don't know why I even came to this ratty ol' place."

Right about then, a scripture suddenly pulled up to the curb inside my head, *"Love one another, as I have loved you. By this shall all men know that you are my disciples."* And I knew what had to be done, something over and above what the woman deserved. Reaching into Sue Jan's style station drawer, I slapped the patented *Trim Snoz* onto my friend's palm. "Your client, your nose hairs."

Sue Jan closed her eyes a moment and looked up at the ceiling. Instantly, I knew she was praying. We like to joke that God is on the ceiling. In this case, one of them low-hanging ceilings with janky tiles always hanging off the brackets.

"Wait, Miz Cornelia." Sue Jan held up the gadget, hand limp with under- enthusiasm. "I got this here battery-operated *Trim Snoz* thingie in my drawer. "If you, ah, have a seat, maybe I can help you with them nose hairs of yours, chop-chop."

The woman eyed Sue Jan warily, but complied, though I'm not sure why. Cornelia sneered my way even as she slunk back into the client chair.

I watched in amazement and awe at what would be remembered as, "The pointy- black-nose-hair incident," began to unfold. Though I knew Sue Jan was weak in the stomach, due to the first-trimester situation, she clicked the gadget on, and set about whirring the *Trim Snoz* into each nasty nostril, talking nonstop as she did. I guessed because of her weak stomach she was trying to psyche herself up instead of "speaking Dutch in a sack" as they say. Based on her last pregnancy, Sue Jan could get nauseous at the drop of a hat.

"It says in the flyer there's a snake charmer, and a sword swallower, and a fire dancer, and an illustrated couple, and a real life midget man magician. There's a yo-yo whiz too. I love yo-yos. Though I never could work one when I was a kid. Always got the thing tangled up around my legs and—"

"You looking for a job?" Cornelia sneered.

Sue Jan put down the trimmer. "What do you mean by that? You know this is my job. I'm co-owner of . . . "

"Circus always needs a fat lady." Cornelia pointed at the two of us and rolled her eyes. "Either one of you girls could moonlight under the big top." She snickered. "Heavens to Murgatroyd! You could wear the big top!"

This time the blood rose to *my* cheeks. I wasn't sure what a Murgatroyd was, but I was certain whatever came out of Cornelia Barlow's mouth couldn't be good.

But Charla, our youngest, and downright sensible stylist calmly put down her scissors and approached the woman. "Ma'am, we're so glad you came here for your beauty needs. And I'm sure you'll agree that in addition to the generous and *free* styling services you received today from Miz Lovita, it was real nice of Miz Sue Jan to take care of them pointy nose hairs of yours too. But right now, I think it would be a good idea for me to walk you to the door. You'd best leave before somebody *Trim Snoz's* them eyebrows of yours right off. You can give them salons in Bentley your business from now on."

But as she helped the woman through the door, Cornelia dragged her feet across the doormat like she'd just stepped on backyard dog dookie. Then she held up her index finger and opened her mouth to speak. "I done shook the dust off my feet and now I'm calling this here place, 'Michelob!'" She pounded the door with her fist as she repeated the word, and then slammed the door behind her so hard the tiny bell on it bounced off the floor.

Sue Jan and I looked at one another. "Michelob?" Sue Jan kept repeating the word, as if saying it over and over would somehow provide the answer. "Ita, you know I've never even tasted alcohol in my entire life, but ain't that some kind of beer? Why's she talking about beer?" She scrunched up her nose.

"What does beer have to do with anything?"

But the hamster wheel in my head was already spinning, and an old sermon Pastor Meeks taught us years ago came back to me. "Hold on a minute! That woman just tried to curse the Crown of Glory and call it 'Ichabod,' only that's a biblical curse from Samuel, First Samuel, I think. It means the glory has left or something like that. It's in the Old Testament and I've heard of it being spoken over churches that are fallen into sin, but never for a beauty salon."

Sue Jan tittered. "Michelob! Hehe, hehe!" She slapped her knees, and slumped over laughing. "That Cornelia's a real pill."

Charla and Jolene and the other clients joined in the laughter. Sue Jan picked up the bell off the floor and giggled. "The expression on that woman's face is—is like a bulldog chewing on a wasp."

I shook my finger. "Now, now, Suey. No need for us to stoop to her level."

"Lovita, if you mean, 'devil-level' you're right, I sure don't want to stoop down to *that* level." Sue Jan had an audience, her favorite situation, and by now *their* sides were splitting. I averted my eyes to the display window instead, mostly to keep myself from giving in and laughing with them. That's when a movement caught my attention. I shuffled to the window for a closer look. "Well, I'll be."

Sue Jan stopped to brush away laugh-tears. "W-what is it, Lovita?"

By then, the sounds had caught up with the sight I'd just seen. I yanked on the cord, pulled the blinds up all the way and cracked open the window. "The circus ain't coming *to* town. It's already here!" The sound of trombones accented my motion as both hairdressers and clients crowded round.

We practically ran over one another trying to get out the door, popping the bell off once again, before we stood on the curb with the rest of the townsfolk. The Wachita business district came to a standstill, with people lining Main Street, mouths gaping at the sight of circus trucks and trailers lumbering past. The last time this many folks were out gawking, Charla and her family had wobbled into town on wonky wheels, sputtering trailer fumes.

A couple of elephants led the parade, each ridden by women in a glittery one-piece bathing-type suit. The women waved, flashing wide red-lipped smiles at the crowd A couple of clowns in teeny-tiny clown cars circled around like ants on a July sidewalk. But when the freak trailer drove by, Sue Jan's mouth dropped like somebody released a trap door. There, peeking out the windows of a special circus truck were a tattooed woman and man. And from what was visible, it looked like every inch of skin was inka-dinka doo'd.

Finally came the largest woman I'd ever seen, sprawled in the back seat of a vintage red Cadillac convertible which hung low on the back end. Either the car was equipped to be a low-rider, or the chassis was bowing under her weight.

The woman grinned and threw kisses like a prom queen from her shiny apple-red lips. And next to her, sitting on the backseat headrest, was a teeny man in a tux waving his itsy-bitsy hands at the crowd. When the woman waved, her arms flapped and rippled back and forth like deflated water wings.

Sue Jan elbowed me in the side. "Lovita, she's—"

I wagged my finger at her. "Now don't say anything you'll regret, Suey."

But she continued, as if she hadn't heard a word.

" . . . She's the most bodacious and big-beautiful woman I've ever seen in my life."

Suddenly, what sounded like a shot rang out. My heart in my throat, I watched as one of the Caddy tires blew and the little man in the penguin suit went flying over the hood.

# CHAPTER TWO

### Three-Ring Circle

"He's breathing." Charla checked for a pulse, but a small blossom of blood slowly expanded under the man's head.

The little man moaned, his teeny voice somehow adorable even under the circumstances. "W-hat happened?"

Sue Jan pulled client wraps off several of our customers and balled them up. Then she gently tucked them around his head to keep him from moving around. "Now set still while we tend to you." She looked up. "Somebody call an ambulance." Jolene pointed to her cellphone. She was already talking to someone. The woman seemed to have a hotline to the hospital ever since she started dating a doctor.

While Sue Jan was doing that, I scampered to help the bodacious, big circus woman out of the car. Not by myself, mind you. I couldn't do any lifting, heavy or not. Crying, the woman was rolling from side to side, trying hard to maneuver herself towards the car door. So I asked a couple of strong Wachita men to come to her rescue. The men pushed and pulled until she finally squeezed through. Once her feet were on the ground, she took off without so much as a thank-you. I tried to lead her by the arm to guide her there, but she pulled away.

A crowd had begun to form around the injured guy, but the woman plowed her way through, her eyes widening at the sight of the man sprawled on the ground. "Max!" Tears streamed down her cheeks. She tried to kneel down next to him, but unless the woman was able to suddenly break all the laws of physics, there was no way *that* was going to happen. Her face turned red and she began to cry out. "Max, oh my Max! Please be okay. You're all I've got now."

Instead of responding though, the injured man's eyelids fluttered, which made me wonder if he was going into shock or something. Sue Jan must have read my mind because she showed up with a bundle of client wraps, kneeled down and covered him. I hadn't even noticed her disappear into the salon to get them.

I figured since the man was riding in the special convertible Caddy, he must've held some kind of special position in the circus. But, regardless of that, it seemed like the man had a place in the woman's heart that was surely bigger than the whole state of Texas.

The second I ventured to pat some reassurance onto the woman's shoulder, the whir of sirens sounded in the distance. "The ambulance is coming." I said, "They'll take good care of him. Do you want us to give you a ride to the hospital?"

She swiped the tears from her eyes and squinted at her cellphone. "Would you? I—I can't believe this is happening. You don't think he's going to die, do you?"

But just then, Sue Jan's cousin's boy, Kenny, burst through the crowd yelling something I couldn't make out at first.

Sue Jan stood. "What's going on Kenny? Why are you creating such a commotion? Don't we have enough happening right now?"

Eyes bulging, he choked out the words. "I caught sight of the gun. Miz Sue Jan."

"What gun?" Sue Jan asked.

"The long gun what shot out the tire on this here Caddy." He pointed up. "The shooter fired from that second story window of your beauty parlor."

Sue Jan's cousin's boy knew what he was talking about. The entire Calhoun clan, natural born hunters and trackers, knew their weapons. If Kenny said he saw a long gun pointed out a window I wouldn't stop one second to doubt the boy.

Sue Jan and I turned to look where he was pointing at the same time. The second floor of the Crown of Glory Beauty Salon and Boutique was no more than an attic storage space. We kept the salon's Christmas decorations up there, along with old client chairs and stuff we didn't have much use for. We hardly ever trudged up the rickety, narrow staircase. Yet, there it was, plain as day. The attic window was open, and the weather-beaten shutters ajar. When Sue Jan and I locked eyes, we both gulped. The two of us are weird like that. Being best friends for so long and all, well, I guess we think and act alike sometimes.

"Kenny," I asked, "did you happen to see who it was who fired the shot?"

He shook his head. "All's I seen was the long gun a-poking out that window."

"Who would do a thing like that?" I spoke out loud what my brain was thinking.

But even as I spoke, a man covered with more ink than a copy machine approached with his own out-loud thoughts.

"Whoever is trying to destroy our circus, that's who," he said, his gargantuan black moustache see-sawing as he spoke.

The bodacious, big lady shot an angry glance at the illustrated man. But he sneered back at her and kept talking loud enough so everyone could hear. "We've had a slew of bad things happen to us circus people. And it's no coincidence." He held his index finger up in the air. "I tell you, we're cursed! Somebody has it in for Mordecai's Circus and Sideshow, and if we don't break this curse, somebody's going to wind up dead."

I found out later that the fellow with all the tats was called Zeke the Freak, his circus moniker. His real name, Ned Turner, didn't sound as circus-y. His wife, Nora went by the name Zara and looked to be tatted up to the same extent. Besides all that, both of 'em were skinny as a couple of meerkats.

There wasn't time enough to listen to him rant though. Sue Jan and I whisked the woman off to the hospital in Sue Jan's van. We had to pull out a seat to fit her. While we were settling the woman in, my mind went into mystery mode. Were Sue Jan and I right in the middle of another mystery? With both of us in a family way, and me almost to term, I wondered if either of us could handle yet another investigation, but mysteries always seemed to find *us*.

I resolved to talk to the tattooed man as soon as possible. He sounded like a disgruntled employee, and disgruntled employees were a wealth of information and possible leads.

So we made it to the hospital, but sure didn't beat the ambulance or anyone else. Wachitians still think like the small-town folk they are, which is why almost all the people who were watching the circus parade crowded into the hospital waiting room and parking lot to hold vigil for the little stranger who sailed over the hood of the car.

The bodacious, big, beautiful woman who was in the car with him was beyond distraught, crying and shaking. Sue Jan and I learned her name was Gerline Whipsnade and she seemed to be the woman in charge of everything. Between tears, she was giving instructions to someone over the cellphone.

"I don't understand why anyone would want to hurt us

## WEIGHTY MATTERS

either." She swiped the tears away. "Yes, we'll need a new tire. Can you take care of that? I have a call in to our insurance guy. Thanks. And would you keep an eye on the elephant's knee? Looks like it's bothering her again. And make sure Trick stays away from the bottle. You know how he gets." She put her phone back in her purse.

"Excuse me," I said. "Gerline, I know we just met and all, and you're in a delicate state right now worrying about your friend, but I couldn't help overhearing what you said about the tires. The police arrived on the scene right when we were leaving. They're still investigating, so I don't think they'll let anyone mess with the crime/accident scene just yet."

"Oh." Her face fell. "I didn't think about that. I—I'm in damage-control mode. I manage the circus. That's what I do."

"You manage the whole enchilada?" Sue Jan asked. "You mean you ain't one of the circus people that perform?"

"People always think that about me because I'm what you call *'zaftig'*. But, in answer to your question, I have a degree in accounting and I minored in business."

Sue Jan held up her index finger. "I don't wanna sound stupid, but I'm gonna have to take the risk. What's a *zaftig*?"

Gerline tilted her head. "It means healthily plump." She sniffed. "But regardless of my size, I'm definitely not the circus fat lady." She winked. "I'm the fat lady who runs the show."

I glanced at Sue Jan, sharing an invisible thought bubble with her. Healthily plump? Who was that woman trying to kid? If Gerline were a trailer home, she'd be a doublewide and then some.

Just then, Dr. Colley lumbered out of the hospital waiting room. "Lumber" is about all the man could manage with his gait. We'd seen a lot of the freakishly-tall doc ever since he and one of our stylists, Jolene McNulty, started dating. They met after he treated her drunk-as-a-skunk son Zane in the ER. But that's a story for another day.

Dr. Colley went straight to the woman, a bleak look on his face. "Miz Whipsnade, my name is Dr. Colley and I've been treating your boyfriend Maxmillian."

"Max." She dabbed away fresh tears. "He goes by Max. Except when he's performing. Then he's 'The Amazing Teeny Carlini.' She cleared her throat. "And he's my fiancé" She thrust a chubby hand to Dr. Colley's face where the stark hospital lights caught the fire and gleam of a large diamond. "See?"

Sue Jan's mouth came unhinged.

"Oh, congratulations." Dr. Colley cleared his throat. "Well, my patient, err, your fiancé, Max," He flipped a page on his chart, "Has a concussion, and I need to keep him here for a couple of days. The fact that he's a . . ."

"Midget," Sue Jan finished.

Dr. Colley corrected, "Little person. Complicates things. So I need to monitor him closely for the next forty-eight hours."

But before the woman could respond, Sue Jan spoke up. "Of course he's little, Dr. Colley. Ain't he a smidget?" She snickered. "That's a mash-up between a smudge and a midget. I made it up myself."

The doctor removed his glasses and stared her down. "Sue Jan, the word "midget" is pejorative. And inventing a word like 'smidget' is insulting. People who are perfectly proportioned like to be called little people. Dwarves are also small but have disproportionate body parts."

Sue Jan's face crinkled like she was confused. "Hmmm, a little person. Like on The Wizard of Oz?" Her eyebrows arched. "At least he ain't a flying monkey."

Gerline snapped back. "Max isn't defined by his size. He's a respected, professional magician who happens to be a little person." She turned her back on Sue Jan and questioned Dr. Colley. "Will he be all right? He—he's not going to die, is he?"

A sob escaped her mouth. "C-can I see him?"

"Of course," he answered. "I'm fairly optimistic about his condition, but as I said, he needs to be monitored overnight, possibly longer."

Gerline shifted her hips like she was preparing to get up, but the chair she was sitting in refused to let go. As a curvy chica myself, I could identify with her predicament. Not that Sue Jan or I have ever been as supersized as her. But we have had a few tangles with lawn chairs in the past. Embarrassing, for sure.

So lickety-split, Sue Jan grabbed one arm of the chair and I grabbed the other while the woman wiggled her bodacious backside out. Not a word was spoken. But both Sue Jan and I could see the gratitude in Gerline's eyes. Though I think she was still kind of mad at Sue Jan. Who could blame the woman?

"I'll take you to see him." Dr. Colley extended an arm to help her up. Gerline continued towards the ER, arm-in-arm with the doctor.

Sue Jan whistled. "Well, I'll be a monkey's uncle. So Gerline's boyfriend is a little tiny Tom Thumb guy, and his name is Max?" She giggled. "His name should be 'Minimum'! Teeheehee. And she's so big and bodacious. What an odd couple. Don't you think so too, Lovita?"

I rolled my eyes. And though reluctant to go along with her, I found myself in a state of guilty-giggling. "Sue Jan, I can't believe I'm going to say this, but I agree with you."

Her eyes widened. "What? You agree with me? That's a first."

I nodded. "Gerline and Max are an odd duo, like a 'Ripley's Believe it or Not' kind of couple."

"But?" she asked, the tone of her voice sounding disappointed. "You sound like you have a big but." She tittered as soon as she realized she said it.

I couldn't help smiling. "Well, I do happen to have a 'big

butt' right now, BUT I'm blaming it on the baby. The 'big but' in our conversation however, is that you were just plain rude to that circus lady and her beau."

"Rude? All I was doing was asking questions. Enquiring minds want to know, you know." Her brows knit together. "Do you really think her supersized panties are in a wad over what I said?"

I nodded even as I laughed. "Yup, I do."

She blew a raspberry on her arm, and spoke, a mocking tone to her voice. "Oh phooey, Lovita! Why do I always put my *zaftig* foot in my mouth? I don't mean any harm. The words always come out all wrong. Nobody understands me."

"Maybe you should take a couple of deep breaths before you say anything. And while you're taking in that air, you could think about what you're going to say. They always tell carpenters to measure twice, cut once. Why not try that with your mouth?"

Sue Jan stuck her tongue out at me. "Lovita, you're a real Smartacus! Why, I'm gonna turn over a new leaf. I'm sick of my mouth getting me into trouble all the time. I'll make sure to apologize to Gerline, and to the whole world of people I've offended in my life. "

"Nice sarcasm." I put my hands on my hips. "You should take this seriously though, Suey, and really think about what I said."

"And pigs should fly, Lovita." She stuck her tongue out again. "But they don't."

# CHAPTER THREE

## Let the Fur Fly

The next day, Sue Jan and I stood in front of Monroe's mayor's desk. Sue Jan and I were there to pick up Monroe for lunch. We decided to find out if the sheriff had made any progress on the circus shooter.

I scanned the room with an eye for all things ugly, and was not disappointed. The mayoral offices were located smack dab in the middle of Wachita, a mere half a block from the salon. Complete with paneling the color of cheddar cheese and nasty shag carpeting in three shades, which happened to be all the colors bananas turn as they rot, the offices looked like the setting for a bad seventies movie. But the crowning *pièce de résistance* in the mayor's office was the bust of Monroe on a faux gold pedestal that Sue Jan had commissioned an "artist" to make for him in Mexico. The bust looked more like Pancho Villa meets the Lucky Charms leprechaun. The artist had seen fit to paint the bust of Monroe in vivid colors, complete with cartoonish hair, rounded myopic eyes and oversized eyeglasses. *Scary.*

"No, I can't go to lunch with you girls today, sweetie." Monroe's expression looked like the definition of sheepish.

"Why not? We planned it and everything." Sue Jan stomped her right foot. "Callie made a special peach pie. She doesn't do that for just anyone, you know. Not anymore."

"Well, I sure am sorry," he ran his right hand palm across his face, "I sure do love peach pie, but I can't leave my desk right now. My phone's been ringing off the hook. Which reminds me–" He held up his palm and pressed the outdated intercom button on his desk. "Mary Jean, please hold all my calls for the next ten minutes, will you? Take messages. Thanks." He took a deep breath. "Okay, besides the accident and the story about somebody shooting the tire out on that car, we've been getting some strange reports."

Sue Jan's eyes grew as wide as I imagined mine were.

"Strange reports?" she asked.

Monroe's face contorted a bit, like he was embarrassed to say what he was going to say. "Reports of some kind of weird-type sightings in the woods around Wachita."

"What?" I asked. "Weird-type sightings? What does that mean?"

Monroe averted his eyes to his desk. He began fiddling with his pen. "The hunters who . . . who reported it swear they saw. They swear they saw a Sasquatch."

"A Bigfoot, right here in Wachita?" Sue Jan tittered. But then all the color in her face drained, which was no small feat because Sue Jan had on a lot of blush. "Around these parts? Ain't them furry creatures up north in them big forests and stuff? What would a hairball like that be doing in Texas? It's too hot for one thing. That old Bigfoot would sweat down to midget size in no time at all. He'd be a 'Littlefoot.'" She grabbed Monroe's collar. "But what I want to know is, are the twins safe? That hairy bully better not mess with my kids or I'll kick his mangy caboose to Tim-buck-too!"

"Now Sue Jan, don't-a, don't go getting all upset. I'm sure

they thought they saw something strange, and it's something else entirely, something completely rational, and easy to explain. Normal, even."

"Speaking of mange. A mangy old bear maybe?" I offered.

He snapped his fingers. "Exactly, Lovita. They could have seen some poor, sick animal and thought they were looking at something entirely different." Monroe looked relieved that I'd suggested a normal-type explanation.

Sue Jan nodded. "But we don't have many bears around here any more. Not since all the so-called progress started up. New buildings and businesses are sprouting up like mushrooms after a storm."

Monroe popped an antacid into his mouth. "There's more. Some folks who found out about the sightings are coming in to investigate." He pulled a handkerchief from his pocket and swabbed his forehead. "One of the hunters called them. And by one of the hunters I mean your cousin, DeWayne."

Sue Jan's face fired up crimson at the mention of her wayward cousin's name.

Monroe went on, voice cracking. "I would have kept things quiet, but now all H-E-DOUBLE TOOTHPICKS is gonna break loose in this town and Wachita is going to be the laughing stock of Texas!" He buried his face in his hands.

I gulped. Once the media got a hold of this juicy bit of news, they'd be crawling all over town hunting for monsters too. "When are they coming?"

He popped his head up like a turtle squinting at the sun. . "They're supposed to come next week, but with all these sightings I'm afraid they'll show up sooner. They're going to film it all. I'm hoping to keep things quiet between now and then. The Bigfoot sightings are probably just a hoax, a practical joke someone is perpetrating on us."

But Sue Jan hadn't heard a thing after the word *film*. "They're bringing a-a film crew?" Sue Jan's eyes glazed over as she floofed her curled-under hair.

"Don't we have enough going on with a circus in town?" I asked. And of course, asking that question reminded me why we stopped in to talk to Monroe in the first place. "Monroe, has your new sheriff made any progress figuring out who took a shot at the circus car?"

Sue Jan laughed. "Circus car, Lovita! Makes me think of one of those teeny tiny clown cars!"

He shook his head. "Not yet. But he's working on it. Sheriff Mel sent the evidence away. They're running ballistics on the bullets Kenny helped them find in the street. Sheriff Mel and his assistant, Deputy Crandall searched your salon attic thoroughly for prints. Feel free to stop in and ask him about what's going on. Tell him I sent you on by. He knows about our town's forensic females and he's agreed to work with you girls." Monroe winked.

"Monroe," I said, "I haven't been formally introduced to either of them yet, but I hope they're a big improvement over the last sheriff you hired."

His head bobbed in agreement. "They're a darn sight better, Lovita. You'll see. They're a good fit for our town."

Sue Jan looked my way. "Well, Lovita, even though my adorable husband can't join us, are you still up for a delicious lunch at Callie's place?" She rubbed her tummy. "The two of us are eating for two, you know."

"Sure thing," I answered. "Can't you hear my stomach growling?"

Five minutes later, we were sitting across from one another in our favorite booth at the Texas Lone Star Café. The place was packed, as usual. It was a good thing we had called ahead and asked Callie to reserve the booth, though originally for three. I would have loved for Hudson, *my* adorable husband, to join us as well, but he'd been working on a very important case all month in and out of town, a case that might one day go to the Supreme Court.

I ordered the chicken-fried chicken with copper penny carrots and rice pilaf on the side. Sue Jan went for the chicken pot pie with a salad on the side. Healthy, for sure, but then again, we knew we were finishing with pie a la mode. And everyone knows pie is a great motivator. In between chomping, we talked about the circus incident.

Sue Jan pointed her fork. "I'm glad Max is gonna be okay. He could have split his head open like a Honeydew."

I nodded. "It's a wonder he wound up with only a mild concussion. Doc says he can go back to work in a day or so as long as he takes it easy."

Sue Jan tee-hee-hee'd. "How hard could it be to pull a bunny out of a hat? I can't wait to see the circus. What time do they open tonight?"

"Five. Hudson's meeting me at the shop. We plan to go every night the show is in town."

"And it's only here for five days." Sue Jan scooped up another forkful of chicken pot pie and shoveled it in her mouth.

I paused, a bite of food on my fork. "We need to talk to that inked-up couple as soon as possible. I'm convinced that fella knows something and is ready to blow some whistles."

"And we need to have a sit-down with Gerline, too." Sue Jan continued. "Somebody either tried to injure Gerline and her Mini Max, or maybe even kill the both of them, depending on how good of a shot they are. Kenny says whoever did it is a decent shot. He told me if that shooter wanted either of them dead, it would have happened."

"So maybe the blown tire was a warning?" I chomped on

another bite of chicken.

"Could be," she shrugged. "But then again, the person who took a potshot at the tire knew Gerline and Max were a-settin' in the back of that Caddy convertible all catawampus, without seatbelts."

"Good point. Maybe the shooter didn't care either way. Dead, alive, or injured." I wiped some rebellious white gravy off the side of my mouth. "The inked-up fella said that a lot of things have been happening."

Sue Jan interrupted. "He said the circus was cursed, to be exact."

"Yeah, I heard that too. But back to reality, maybe—just maybe—someone has a beef with the circus or the people who run it."

We pointed at one another and spoke in sync. "Gerline and Max!"

"Jinx!" Sue Jan's eyes widened. "When you say the exact same thing at the same time you have to say, 'the king of France wet his pants right in the middle of a ballroom dance!'"

Sue Jan swiped her last bite of pie between her lips and pointed her fork at me. "Lovita, I have an idea. Let's go round to the circus and pay 'em a visit. We need to do some recon. That's military talk for 'reconnaissance.'"

I blinked. "Wow, you're using some fancy words."

"I been studying up on the right-sounding words to use in our forensic female profession, and that one's a winner." Sue Jan reached into her purse, pulled out some cash and dropped it on the table. "My treat this time, Lovita. Your turn next, okay?"

I nodded. "You got it, super sleuth sister."

We paid for our meal and then headed down the block to Sue Jan's Mommy Loser Kiddy Cruiser, but just as Sue Jan put the key in the ignition, a man's voice sounded from the way-back-seat. And the hairs on my head tingled a silent alarm.

## WEIGHTY MATTERS

"Don't go crazy or nothing. I ain't here to hurt you. I'm here to tell you something important—"

But before he could continue, Sue Jan started whacking the man over the head with an umbrella she always kept next to her in the front seat.

"Yeouch!" The tattooed dude rubbed the top of his head, his face and gigantic mustache scrunched into a crumple that reminded me of a dead rodent.

"It's you!" I recognized the tatted man.

Sue Jan, umbrella raised in mid-air, yelled. "What are you doing in my van, Inka-Dinka-Do?"

The man held out his arms. "Please don't hit me no more. I heard you two were detective chicks so I come to talk to you about something important, but I didn't want nobody to see me talking to you. Too dangerous."

I reached over to stay Sue Jan's arm. "Dangerous? Do you—do you feel threatened?"

"Who cares how he feels? I sure feel threatened by a strange man in my car!" Sue Jan glared.

And my friend was right. I was as creeped out as my friend, but the intense curiosity I was feeling seemed to counteract my fear, although I did make a mental note to lock all doors, both to home and vehicle from now on. Wachita wasn't the same little town where folks could be trusted to do what's right.

"I—I'm sorry. I should have thought about a better way to meet with you. The wife's always telling me I should think before I act."

I looked over at Sue Jan and she immediately lowered the umbrella. She stared at the stranger. "So what's your name, Etch-a-Sketch?"

Sue Jan and I already knew the man's name because we'd asked around, but my friend was employing a forensic female move: Ask 'em the obvious and compare notes.

He cocked his head to the side. "Name's Ned Turner. But I go by Zeke the Freak. Call me Zeke. And my wife's Zara."

I rested my arms on the headrest. "Well Zeke, what's on your mind?"

He glanced from Sue Jan to me. "If you want to call me Ned in private you can, but just be sure to call me Zeke if you see me in public, okay?"

"We're calling you Zeke. It rhymes with freak, which makes it easy to remember, especially because we're a little freaked out right now. Now flap your jaw." Sue Jan ordered.

Flap your jaw? That expression made me wonder if my friend had been taking in too many 1940s detective movies. I resolved to ask her about that later.

Eyes wide, the man leaned forward. "Someone's trying to bring down the circus."

I could practically hear his heart thumping out of his chest. "Why?" I asked.

Sue Jan added, "Yes, tell us how you came to that conclusion."

I noticed Sue Jan had a small pad in one hand and a pencil in the other hand poised above it.

"It started with Gerline's father dying under mysterious circumstances." He gulped. "Trystan was the circus ringmaster, and a good one at that. You'd never meet a nicer man."

"Can you repeat that? His name was Twisting?" Sue Jan asked. She flicked her tongue on the edge of the pencil before starting to write. "That's bizarro. What kind of parents would name their kid that? And I thought I had bad parents."

He blinked. "No, it's Trystan." Zeke spelled it out. "T-r-y-s-t-a-n."

She shook her head, "If you say so. There are some real oddball names out there."

He scrunched his nose. "It's not that odd. In fact, if you go to

England—"

Sue Jan held up her pencil. "Okay, okay. Let's stick to the topic, Stranger Danger."

He opened his mouth to say something back, but I simultaneously elbowed Sue Jan and stopped her before she could get a word out. Good thing too, because Sue Jan was going for the man's jugular time and again. We'd never get anything useful out of the intruder if she kept attacking him.

"How'd he die and how long ago?" I asked.

"Almost a year ago. A ballast bag hit him on the head. We use sandbags as counterweights in the tent over the main ring, similar to a theater stage. And that's where it happened." He continued. "Right on the mark."

"What do you mean by 'the mark'?" Sue Jan questioned.

"On stage. I mean, in the ring. There's a mark where a performer is supposed to stand. And that's where he stood when it fell on his head. Anyway, that's what we call it."

I snapped my fingers. "So you're saying someone knew exactly where the man was going to stand and rigged up that sandbag so it would fall smack dab on Trystan's head."

"Crushed his top hat like an accordion," he nodded. "And-and his skull too. But not so much like an accordion. More like a—"

Sue Jan eyed him with disgust. "We get it. We get it. What else you got?"

He folded his arms and leaned back. "Madame Curio."

"Who's that?" she asked.

"She's a fortune-teller."

"Does she wear one of them turbans and ba-jankly earrings on her ears?"

"She does and she's almost as big but not quite near as big as Gerline."

Sue Jan giggled. "So you're telling us she's a four-chin teller?" She snorted at her own joke.

Zeke tightened his lips together, obviously not amused. "I guess that's one way of putting it, Mrs. Mayor Lady. She's a good gal and she almost died from food poisoning. That's what the doctor said he thought it was. But nobody else got sick from eating the same food. Oh, and I almost forgot, that same day the ringmaster died, Johnny Roo was trying to tighten a loose tent flap in storm winds when a tent stake snapped in half and flew up. Almost hit him. We examined it afterwards. A metal tent stake sawed almost in half. It was an accident waiting to happen. Or a so-called accident."

"Is that it?" Sue Jan scribbled. "You got anything else?"

Zeke ran his sleeve across his jaw. "Ain't that enough?"

"What my friend is trying to say is, aren't those events easy to explain? All these things can be explained except for the shooting incident."

"What about Dixie? She's one of our trapeze artists and she about fell to her death from a frayed rope. If it weren't for the safety net, she'd have been flying with the angels."

"Now that's interesting." I leaned towards Sue Jan. "You have to admit that all this stuff combined smells fishier than the dumpster behind Long John Silver's."

Sue Jan grunted.

Zeke put his inked-up hands together in a church-and-steeple clasp. "But that ain't all." He gulped. "You're gonna think I belong in the looney bin if I tell you more."

*As if our thoughts weren't already on that track.* Nevertheless, I shook my head and elbowed Sue Jan to do likewise. "No, no we won't," I said. "She and I have seen a lot of strange things in this here town. You-a, you wouldn't believe half the things we've come across."

He closed his eyes and spoke. "L-last night a couple of us thought we saw something around the big tent. Right at dusk, a dark shape against the horizon. At first we thought it might be a bear." His breath quickened. "But the way it stood upright was strange. And the fur was different from a bear's. And it smelled real bad too. Not that bears smell real good, but this smell was in a class by itself. I think we must have been downwind of it."

"What was it?" I asked.

His jaw tightened as if he was deciding whether or not to say something.

"For goodness sake, and tell us *what* you saw!" Sue Jan ordered.

Zeke's eyes flew open. "Whatever it was, it ran off real fast. Faster than any bear I've ever seen."

Eyes riveted on the man, I asked, "If it wasn't a bear, what was it?"

Zeke's hands clamped onto the bucket seat. "A big hairy monster. I know it sounds crazy, but I think we seen a Bigfoot!"

# CHAPTER FOUR

## A Hairy Mess

Another Bigfoot sighting was too much of a coincidence to ignore. Sue Jan called Monroe to let him know, but the news brought the already downcast mayor down so low I doubt the man could have crawled under a pregnant ant. I could tell by the way the man sighed on the speakerphone. My instinct told me there was some kind of connection between the circus and Sasquatch, but proving that link was going to be one 'hairy' situation.

"C'mon, Lovita." Sue Jan gestured me forward. "You and I are gonna meet some of these circus folk. We got to get to the bottom of all this. Attempted murder is one thing, but Bigfoot sightings just set this investigation on fire!"

"How do you suppose we're going to do that?" I asked. "They're not letting anyone through the gate yet. The first show is tonight."

"Pshaw." Sue Jan rolled her eyes. "Don't be silly, Lovita. You're with a VIP. I'll git us in. Wait and see."

After our weird conversation with Zeke, Sue Jan had insisted we hightail it over to the circus grounds to do some serious sleuthing. Jolene and Charla covered for us at the Crown of Glory as usual. Sue Jan didn't have to worry about the kids during workdays. She and Monroe had hired a nanny to take care of the twins. And my adorable housetrained Yorkie, Buttercup was content to snooze and roam the house chewing on bones or playing with toys. So we felt free to snoop, but where to start?

Two men on unicycles worked the curious crowd near the entrance, handing out flyers that announced the first show.

Sue Jan tugged at one of the unicyclist's shirttails, almost causing him to lose his balance. He pulled out the cigar plug from his mouth and stared at her, bracing one foot on the ground, dangerously close to a pile of smelly animal do-do.

"Whadduya want, lady?"

"My name is Sue Jan Madson, and I'm the mayor's wife of this here town you're camped in, and," she gestured, "this is my best friend and business partner, Lovita Mae Taylor. And we would love to have a private tour of the circus and talk with Gerline too. Lovita and I have already been acquainted with her at the hospital. We drove her there, you know. After the accident." She opened her eyes wide. "Or crime."

*I should have known Sue Jan would play the mayor's wife card.*

His eyes widened at the word "crime," and he leaned down to pick up his unicycle. Frankly, I was surprised at how tall the man was when he stood up. Towering at almost seven feet!

"Follow me," he said, in an instructional-video kind of monotone.

When I turned around I noticed a bit of reddish fluff on the back of his shirt and held it between my fingers. When he turned, I held it up and twirled it around. "You had something, something on your back."

He squinted at me. "Hmmph. Thanks."

When he turned back around Sue Jan gave me the thumbs up.

She followed him, and I followed her, past a line of tents and vehicles and wild animal smells. I drew up next to my friend as she gulped and realized her face suddenly looked greener than gourd guts.

*That first trimester thingy.* "You okay, Suey?" I asked.

She pressed her lips together and nodded in a very unconvincing way. "Um, hmm."

The cigar man rang a little bell hanging on a string outside a travel trailer.

"Who is it?" A woman's voice called out in response.

He climbed the three steps, knocked on the trailer door and stuck his head in. "It's Trick. I got some women who want to talk to you. One of 'em says she's the mayor's rib and she knows you."

"Send them in."

Sue Jan looked at me, one brow raised.

Right in front of us, sitting behind a little TV tray, was Gerline, the bodacious, big, beautiful woman we'd met. She looked a darn sight better today than her frayed state at the hospital. Her hair was straight, black and shiny as a crow's wing. And the woman's skin was all glow-y and beautiful. I watched as she struggled to her feet.

She held out her hand to each of us. "Well, hello there ladies. Good to see you again. Have a seat. Sorry about the folding chairs, but we're a mobile community."

When we'd finished saying our hellos, I asked, "When is the doc sending Max home?"

Gerline sighed. "Dr. Colley wants to keep him another day, maybe two. I understand his reasoning, but I sure miss my man and I want him back. And besides that, we're supposed to perform tonight. Circus performers work under the strict credo that 'the show must go on.' If Max was out of that hospital, he'd be performing no matter what condition he was in." Her brow raised, "But since he won't be here, I'll be filling in as the ringmaster, something my father always wanted me to do anyway."

My interest piqued, I couldn't help asking. "So why aren't you doing the ringmaster thing now instead of Max?"

Gerline raised her shoulders. "I don't know. I guess because Max is really passionate about doing it."

But the expression on her face told me there was more to that story. "That's not the only reason, is it?" I realized I'd tilted my head as soon as the words came out. So much for the calm detached detective persona I was going for.

"I'm too much woman to stand up for that long." A tear formed in the corner of only one eye. "I've always been voluptuous." She rustled a Chinese hand fan open and began to wave the painted silk back and forth near her face. The fragrance of cedar filled the air.

Sue Jan and I exchanged knowing looks, but Sue Jan spoke up. "Girlfriend, we get that. As two big, bodacious, beautiful ladies to another big, bodacious, beautiful lady, we know exactly how you feel."

The woman touched the fan to her chest. "Exactly how I feel?" She leaned her head back and giggled. "Excuse me for saying so, but you girls aren't exactly voluptuous." She drew the fan together and pointed. "I'm guessing you two are always on some kind of diet, right?"

"When we're not pregnant, you bet." I laughed.

Gerline looked from one to the other of us. "So you're both pregnant? Isn't that cute!" She stared at my belly. "I should have guessed."

"Maybe if you got on an exercise plan, you could lose enough weight to be the ringmaster," Sue Jan offered, a helpful lilt to her voice. "Me and Lovita have lost weight before and we plan on doing it again after these babies are born."

The woman threw back her head and laughed. "Why would I do that? I love the way I look. And my man worships the 'Rubenesque' form as the ideal woman. He loves being seen with me, especially at the beach." She winked.

I wished she hadn't said that because from that point on I had a picture in my head that I couldn't shake, that of a Teeny Carlini ogling her flabulousness in a teeny bikini at the beach.

Hands on her hips, Sue Jan snapped back. "If by Rubenesque you mean you been eating one too many Rueben sandwiches, I'm not gonna argue with that." Without waiting for an answer, she continued. "Hey, hate to go off subject, but I've got a couple of questions for you, Gerline. Why is this circus called Mordecai's? Your last name is Whipsnade. And, why did that fellow call me the mayor's rib."

Gerline answered. "In response to your first question, Mordecai was the previous owner of this circus. Unfortunately, it's expensive to change all the signage. In time though, I plan to. And as for the second question, that fellow's name is Trick, and what he said references Adam and Eve. Get it?"

Sue Jan giggled as if she understood, but I could tell she had no idea what the woman was talking about. I resolved to explain the joke to her later. For now there were more important things to be done.

The woman shuffled some papers on her desk. "Now what brings you girls here today," she winked, "besides the obvious magic of the circus?"

I swallowed too fast and started to cough. "We're here—we're—we're here to find out who's trying to kill you and/or Max and destroy Mordecai's Circus and Sideshow."

Her mouth fell open, but she responded in an odd way, by sinking her fingers into a bowl full of candy, like one of those claw machines at Walmart. She hoisted the chocolate to her mouth in between sentences. "Since you put it that way, I'm all ears. I'll do what I can to help, of course. I'll do anything to help. This situation has me, has us all, rattled. I heard what Zeke told you at the scene of the accident, but I can assure you, the circus is not under any kind of curse. That's a ridiculous concept. Silly, even. I probably shouldn't be telling you this, but Zeke is an out-there kind of guy, if you know what I mean. I hope I'm explaining myself well."

I studied her face. Suddenly, the 'cool as a cuke' businesswoman was starting to blabber. *Interesting.*

Sue Jan broke in. "Gerline, pardon my French, but that's cuckoo for Cocoa Puffs! That incident was no accident. Someone aimed a gun and took a couple of shots at you or your vehicle. You could have died. Your boyfriend, *err,* fiancé could have died, or even some 'rando' person could have died in the crowd from a stray bullet. Whoever did this has some kind of beef either with you, or your boyfriend, or the circus."

Gerline froze, fingers slick with chocolate mid-air. "Fiancé. He's my fiancé." She put the candy down and wiped her hands on a napkin. "This is rather personal, but I suppose I have to tell you since I get the feeling that you two don't give up easily." She tried to smile, but he lips sagged into a frown. "The truth is that I've been upset and distraught, maybe even depressed since my father . . ."

Sue Jan narrowed her eyes. "Of course you are. Who wouldn't be? We're real sorry about what happened. And please, please excuse me for asking this, but just how did he kick the bucket?"

I had to admire my friend for asking what we already knew or thought we knew. We absolutely had to hear Gerline's version of events.

The woman dabbed at her eyes with a vintage floral handkerchief.

"It was an accident. Someone didn't fasten a ballast bag the right way and it, well, the heavy bag of sand fell from the tent ceiling and struck him on the head." She sobbed. "The EMS people told me he died instantly, but that's hardly comforting to hear."

"What a horrible way to go! I'm so sorry. How terrible for you." I worked up my courage. "Who was supposed to, uh, see to that sort of thing? Was there someone responsible?"

She cast her eyes downward. "At first everyone thought it was Johnny."

"Roo?" Sue Jan asked.

"That's right." Gerline patted her eyes with the handkerchief. "But he was busy trying to tie down a tent flap. There was a big storm coming and the wind was cracking the flap so hard it sounded like a lion tamer's whip. I could hear it from my trailer. Normally, Johnny would have checked and rechecked everything before the show like he always does, but not that day. The job fell to his backup."

"Who?" I asked.

"Pickles."

"Pickles?"

"He's a clown."

"With a name like Pickles, I hope so," I smiled.

"We all help out when there's a job to be done. Everybody's familiar with setup and takedown in a small operation like this. And Pickles, well he used to 'rag out,' you know, what Johnny does, only for a different circus. But Pickles had a bit of a drinking problem and the other circus canned him."

"And you hired him?" I asked.

"My father hired him as a clown, not a roustabout. He had a soft spot for circus people. That's why they all loved him." Her voice trailed off. "Almost all."

Sue Jan zoomed in at full throttle. "Pickles was pickled? So do you think what happened was his fault? Was he sloshed? Not that I'm saying he did it on purpose. If he wasn't drunk, maybe he was rusty at that sort of thing and forgot how to tie knots the right way or secure stuff. On the other hand, if he was *loco in cabeza* because of the booza, then he would be directly responsible for your father's demise. Ain't that right?"

Gerline's voice cracked. "I wish—"

Sue Jan squinted like she was confused. "All I'm saying is, maybe we can help you find out."

"—he wasn't dead," she finished.

"Pickles is—is dead?"

Sue Jan and I did it again. In my head, I repeated the King of France line knowing all the while that my friend was doing likewise. At the same time that was happening, the hairs on my arms reared up at the news. Out of all the other incidents Zeke had told us about during his surprise visit, the man had failed to mention Pickles or the fact that the clown was now in a permanent cucumber slumber. And that was a big dill.

# CHAPTER FIVE

■■■■■■■■■■■■■■■■■■■■■■■■■

## Jumping Through Hoops

Gerline told us that Pickles had disappeared shortly after the homicide. His body, in full-on clown makeup and costume, was found on a dirt logging-road less than a mile away from where the circus was at the time. Which told me one very important thing—the real murderer was still out there somewhere. Maybe Pickles was a pawn used to carry out the dirty deed. Whether the clown knew what he was doing or not, the mastermind behind the deed made sure that Pickles had beeped his last horn.

After leaving Gerline's tent, Sue Jan and I whispered our suspicions to one another and decided our next move would be to ultimately find and speak to Zeke and Zara. Unless of course we happened upon Johnny Roo, Madame Curio, or Dixie first . . .

And as it happened, we did spot Johnny Roo. He was securing a tent peg with a huge mallet. When I saw him with his shirt off, sweat glistening off his rippled abs, I was dazzled. Until Sue Jan gently poked me in the side with her elbow.

"Lovita, don't let yourself be hypnotized by this man's amazing sweaty muscular body. Snap out of it and remember who you are—a forensic female! Plus you're married and out-to-here," she gestured, "preggies."

I blinked. Sue Jan was really stepping up, in every way, to the task of investigating this convoluted carny crime scene. Of course it helped that she'd solved a fruitcake crime all on her own over Christmas while Hudson and I were visiting his side of the family in England. "Thanks, I guess seeing this man's amazing sweaty muscular body made me realize how much I miss my husband, that's all."

"When's he coming home, again? I know you told me, but I forgot," Sue Jan whispered.

"He'll be home later this afternoon, and in time for the circus performance for sure."

She winked. "Good. Now let's go talk to this circus hunk and get on with this investigation."

I cleared my throat. "You're Johnny Roo, right?"

He put down his mallet and stood up, tipping his hat as he did. "All day."

I cleared my throat. "Would you mind if we asked you a few questions? Gerline said it would be all right."

He glanced toward Gerline's trailer. "She did, did she? Well then, I guess anything Gerline says goes around here."

Johnny gestured to a collection of old soda crates and limped surprisingly fast over to where they were. He set out one for each of us under the shade of an old cottonwood tree, positioning his in front of the trunk. When he sat, he leaned back against the tree and groaned. "Sorry. Feels good on my back."

"I'll bet." Sue Jan stumbled over her words. "Don't you want to put on a shirt? We-we-we could wait."

He smirked. "I'll be getting right back to work after this little conversation, so if you don't mind, I'll remain shirtless."

"Oh, okay, no problem. We get it." Sue Jan tittered.

I knew by the way she tittered that she was as *uber*-uncomfortable as I was.

Sue Jan pointed to his leg. "And excuse me for saying so, but I couldn't help noticing you have a limp. How did that happen?"

Johnny stared back at her a moment, then proceeded to roll up his pants leg revealing a prosthetic limb.

"I lost my leg to a killer whale off the coast of New Guinea back in '82. I'll never forget that day. The water was calm, like glass. And out of nowhere, this big fish come for my leg. Took it in one gulp." He snapped his finger. "Like that!"

Sue Jan jumped back. "Whoa, that—that's scary. I'll bet that hurt real bad."

"That it did, Miss." He reached down to caress the prosthetic. "Sometimes I still feel my missing leg. Doctors call it phantom pains. Ghost limb." He grinned. "So, when my girlfriend saw what happened to me she took off and left me for good. Broke off our engagement. I healed up and had to look for a new job, so I joined the circus and the folks here nicknamed me Johnny Roo 'cause I hopped around at first like a kangaroo. Get it?" He explained, "This prosthetic was uncomfortable in the beginning. Took a while for me to get used to the thing, but I finally did. I stopped hopping and started limping. Ain't that dandy? So ladies, there you have it. The story of how I lost my leg, my livelihood, my girl, and my life. Are we done here?" He rose stiffly and took a few steps away from us. "I have work to do and it ain't gonna get done by itself."

I called after him. "I understand that you were working on a special project, trying to fix a tent flap the day Trystan died. Did you feel the same way about Trystan that you do about Gerline?"

He scowled. "If it wasn't for Trystan, I'd be dead. He took me under his wing and gave me a reason to live." His voice cracked, "If I could go back to the day of the accident, I would give my other leg to save his life. Gerline's his daughter and I'm loyal to her like I was loyal to him. You satisfied now?"

I took a deep breath. "Sorry Johnny. We didn't mean to touch a nerve. But we believe that Trystan's death is suspicious and that there's a good chance he might have been murdered."

He glared at us, but came back and sat on the crate. "Duh! Everyone knows the clown did it."

"Maybe," I nodded, "but how do you explain Pickles' death?"

"The sheriff said it was a cardiac arrest that killed him. And as far as I'm concerned, he deserved it. They called it divine retribution, and that's all right with me."

"What if it wasn't? The story is all too tidy. What was his motive? Gerline told us that her father gave Pickles a job after he was fired. Do you think Pickles would repay that kindness by murdering him?"

He licked his lips like he was thinking. "No. I never thought about it that way. Just figured God evened the score with Pickles dying the way he did, so sudden and all."

"Sudden and convenient," Sue Jan added.

I continued my questioning. "Did Pickles like Trystan? Was there any reason to believe he had a problem with him?"

Johnny shook his head. "No, Pickles never said a bad word about the boss."

"Then why is it so easy to believe that he murdered the man? But even if Pickles did it, and I'm not saying he did, he didn't act alone. Someone else had to be in on the deed and whoever it was might have considered Pickles expendable."

Sue Jan drew a finger across her neck and screeched to get the point across. "We're real sorry for your loss. Your boss obviously meant something to you. From what we've heard so far, the man was pretty much well-liked by everyone."

Johnny closed his eyes. "Except for one."

"Who?"

"The man who couldn't pay his gambling debt and had to turn over the circus to him."

Sue Jan threw her head back and let out a whistle. "Bingo!"

Who knew? Apparently, it's considered bad luck to whistle in a circus before a performance. Or eat peanuts, which Sue Jan did when she heard the line about the man who lost the circus in a card game. While she was apologizing for the whistle incident, she pulled out the bag of peanuts from her purse and started cracking 'em open. Another bad luck thingie. From that moment on, Sue Jan was double-trouble as far as the circus folk were concerned. We felt about as welcome as a hair on a biscuit.

But in spite of her new status, we were able to duck into Madame Curio's colorful gypsy wagon before word got to her. Of course Sue Jan made an interesting point. If the woman was a fortune-teller, she should have already known.

My mind was still stuck on the gambling angle, a sure-fire motive for many a dirty and dastardly deed. But I tucked it away until I could devote some serious thought to it.

Madame Curio's mini gypsy wagon was decorated with all kind of mystical stuff of the cheap variety, the junky kind of stuff you'd find at a Party Central store marked down after Halloween. Her "crystal ball" was nothing more than an old glittered-up Christmas snow globe.

"Welcome ladies!"

I did a double take when I saw her. Zeke sure wasn't kidding about Madame Curio's size. Although she was sitting at a small table, the one with the crystal ball, I could see she was about the same size as Gerline, but with more exotic looks, namely wavy black hair, pale skin and blue eyes.

Madame Curio puffed on a thin cigar, her gemstone eyes following our every move. She motioned us to sit on two rough benches built into the sides of the wagon. "Tea?" She plucked a teapot from a small camp stove and poured the steaming liquid into a demitasse cup. Brownish tea leaves rose with the liquid all the way to the rim.

Sue Jan and I shook our heads.

"Cookie?" She gestured to a plate of downright delicious-looking cookies, about half a plate actually. From the crumbs on the sides of Madame Curio's lips, I could see she'd already sampled them. Sue Jan, already mesmerized by the plate, had utilized her gift for cookie radar. I gave Suey a 'snap out of it' kind of look as I nudged her. We had to focus on the investigation. "Thanks for asking, but no thanks," I said.

She shrugged. "Suit yourself. Now what can Madame Curio do for you today?" She raised the cigar high in the air, the smoke creating a magical, though polluted ambience. "I see the future. I see the past, and everything in between. Is someone talking about you? Or are you looking for love? Need a good job? Are you sick? Do you trust your boyfriend? Madame Curio sees all!" She broke into a fit of coughing.

Sue Jan opened her mouth first. After all, this woman might be the only circus person who would ever talk to her again. "Howdy Madame."

The woman raised her hand. "Please," she looked around like a vice squad was crouching outside the windows, "don't shorten my name. Call me by my full name, puh-lease!"

Sue Jan's mouth formed a perfect "O." All right-y then, *Madame* Curio. My name's Sue Jan and this is Lovita. I'm the mayor's wife of this here town, and me and my best friend, Lovita are business partners. We would like to ask you a few questions if you wouldn't mind."

The woman's mouth opened like a hinge into a smile of sorts. "But of course. That's what I'm here for, to answer your questions." The tiny metal discs on her polyester headscarf jangled as she moved. "However, I too am a businesswoman and my time is precious to me." She rested the back of her hand on the wobbly table, palm open.

I elbowed Sue Jan and whispered. "I think she wants some money. Got any cash? I've got five bucks on me."

"Okay, hand it over." Sue Jan snatched the bill from my hand and laid it to rest in the woman's palm. Then she settled into the folding chair and pointed at the snow globe. "But you won't be needing that thing."

Madame Curio scrunched her shoulders. "You want to know who took a potshot at Teeny Carlini, right?"

Sue Jan's face lost all color. "Yes, but how did you—?"

"Word travels fast in the circus. Also, you're lucky I'm even talking to you after you whistled and ate peanuts before the performance. You seem surprised that I heard about it. I told you, Madame Curio sees all! And then I told myself, 'this woman, she's an outsider. How would she know the rules and the taboos and the circus superstitions?' So here I am talking to you." Bracelets jangling, she held out her palm again.

Sue Jan reached into her purse, elbow-deep, and pulled out another five. "What do you know?"

The woman pursed her lips. "The little rascal has a lot of enemies. The shooter could have been anyone."

Sue Jan and I both pushed back on our chairs when she spoke.

"Teeny Carlini? Maxa-Mini has enemies?" Sue Jan winked, her voice booming.

"Shhhh." The woman held an index finger to her mouth. "The only one who likes him is Gerline, and nobody can understand why. Max is a real pepper sprout with absolutely no filters or the slightest bit of tact out of his mouth. Plus, he has poor social skills and a chip on his little shoulder." Madame Curio dipped a spoon into her cup and fished out most of the leaves before taking a sip.

"You're saying that anyone, or everyone in this circus, with the exception of Gerline has some kind of grumble with him?" I asked.

The four-chin teller wiggled her oversized fingers. Sue Jan peeled another fiver out of the wallet she fished from the bottom of her huge purse.

"Exactly." She wiggled her fingers again.

Sue Jan's face scrunched into a scowl. "Listen up Chica, even copywriters don't get five dollars a word. Speak up."

"Oh, all right." The woman settled back in her chair, which squeaked and creaked in response.

"What do you know about Trystan's death?" I asked. "We heard you got food poisoning."

Madame Curio's face froze. "I-I don't know anything about Trystan's, I mean about his-his death. But I know I've never had food poisoning. My stomach is like cast iron." She patted her belly, and then pointed her index finger to the sky. "I was poisoned."

"What?" Sue Jan questioned.

"Somebody left a tray of cookies on this table. I assumed they were from a fan. Believe it or not, stuff like that happens a lot, especially when I tell a favorable fortune. Or they could have been from a secret admirer." She winked. "That happens too."

"And you ate them?" she asked.

"Are you kidding me? Homemade thumbprint cookies with raspberry jam? You bet I did. But about ten minutes later, I started feeling sick and 'tossed my cookies,' so to speak. After that, I drank a lot of water and felt better. But I was still kind of weak for a couple of days after. Not myself at all. It's a good thing I do my job sitting down or I wouldn't have been able to work."

"If you think somebody tried to poison you, why are you eating those cookies?" I pointed to the tray. "Did you bake them yourself?" I asked.

She flicked ash from her smelly stinky petite cigar and smiled. "Those cookies are from someone I know."

"Oh . . ." I sighed. "Well since you ate the evidence, the ones that made you sick, we'll never know if the other cookies were tainted."

Sue Jan narrowed her eyes. "How can you be so sure the other cookies were tainted?"

Madame Curio pointed to her temple. "Because I'm a psychic, remember?"

Sue Jan folded her arms. "Then I guess you already know who did it." She turned to me, "Lovita, we might as well close up shop on this case 'cause this here woman's got all the answers."

Madame Curio shook her head. "I-I didn't say that. I just know that somebody tried to kill me and I don't think they're done trying."

"Why would anyone want to kill you?" I asked.

"Because."

"Because of what?"

She coughed. "Because I might have seen something that day. Because I-I did see something—"

Madame Curio paused. Was she trying to decide whether or not to tell us? Though I wasn't sitting on the edge of my seat, I suddenly felt like I was.

"Cat got your tongue?" Sue Jan leaned in. "Tell us what you saw that day."

She didn't answer. Just stared back at us with a surprised kinda look in her eyes. At first I thought Madame Curio had a real flair for drama. The woman started waving her arms full of jingly-jangly bracelets in the air. But neither one of us realized something was wrong until the woman started clutching her throat with both hands as she struggled to breathe.

I jumped up and attempted the Heimlich maneuver on the woman right at the table, which was no easy feat between my protruding stomach and her vastness. Sue Jan was already on the cellphone calling for help.

Helpless, I watched as the woman toppled to the floor like a felled tree. Somehow, I managed to crouch down next to her, settling on my hands and knees. Her skin had a grey cast and I noticed her lips were turning blue. Madame Curio grabbed a clump of my hair, drawing me close. Her lips moved and with her last shallow breath, the woman determined to squeak out a word next to my right ear.

"Silver . . ."

# CHAPTER SIX

■ ■ ■ ■ ■ ■ ■ ■ ■ ■ ■ ■ ■ ■ ■ ■ ■ ■ ■ ■ ■ ■ ■ ■ ■ ■

## Cracking the Whip

Silver? What was Madame Curio trying to tell us with her last smoke-y breath? Hide the silver? Polish the silver? Behind every cloud is a silver lining? Why would she say something like that in the middle of dying?

Sue Jan and I had snapped into action to try and save her life, but it was obvious to both of us and to the paramedics that the poor woman was gone pecan. The body count was starting to pile up like empty Pixie Sticks at a Pork-Rind-and-Pixie-Sticks party. Besides the attempted murder of Max, there were a string of actual deaths. First Trystan the ringmaster, followed by Pickles the clown, and now Madame Curio the fortune-teller!

The opening night performance of the circus was of course, postponed out of respect, but only for a day. I guess circus folk can't afford to grieve too long. The poor woman would be buried before the circus departed Wachita at the end of the week.

Sue Jan and I managed to speak with Dr. Colley and he told us he was pretty sure Madame Curio died of a cardiac arrest. But Mel Wilkes, the nice new sheriff, promised to let us know what the coroner in Bentley told him about the cause of death. He was banking on the cookies. Sue Jan and I had our own theories though. I said it was something in the tea. But Sue Jan swore it had to be the skinny smelly cigar. The sheriff told us they were testing them all. Whatever the cause, Madame Curio sure went fast. Her passing reminded me of the way my own daddy died, right at the kitchen table. Dead before the toast popped up.

"Is Hudson back yet?" Sue Jan peered at me from the driver's seat, her eyes ringed in red. She pulled up in front of the Crown of Glory.

I sniffled and swiped at my eyes. "He texted me. Got back about an hour ago. I texted him all the details."

She glanced toward the salon. "Go home, Lovita. You need to be with your husband. I can tell that this—this horrible situation really got to you today. I'll take care of your clients. Heaven knows I owe you."

"But it, this must have gotten to you too, Suey."

She looked down. "Of course it did, but I'm not as bad off as you. That's what happens in the last part of your pregnancy. You get super-emotional. The first trimester has nothing on the last."

I pulled out a tissue and threaded it between my hands. "You know what got to me the most?"

"No . . ."

"S-she was so huge. When I looked at her, it's like I had a glimpse of what people saw when they looked at me all these years."

"At *us*. You and I wear the same size clothes, remember? Except right now. You're way more pregnant." She tried to smile, but her lips quivered.

"Anyway, when I saw her die, I thought, 'that could be me one day.' What if I allow myself to get that big and I die and

Hudson has to raise our child alone? Madam Curio looked to be around our same age. And now she's dead."

"She was probably murdered," Sue Jan argued.

"Or not." I shook my head. "Even if she did meet with foul play, her weight was killing her slowly and surely. You can't deny that."

"No argument here."

"Today was a defining moment for me, one I don't think I'll ever forget. I'm going to start now. Eating for two isn't a license to pig out all the time. And after I have my baby, I'm really going to get serious about losing weight and exercising and keeping me and my family healthy."

Sue Jan placed her hands over mine. "All for one, and one for all!"

"We're only two musketeers."

"No we're not!" Sue Jan grinned. "Counting the babies, there are at least four of us. That makes four musketeers." She rubbed her belly. "Unless I'm carrying twins again. Hah! And what are the odds of that happening?"

I laughed. "For anyone else, astronomical. For you, the odds might be pretty good."

She tapped my arm. "Or the goods are odd. Now shush, Lovita and go home."

"Are you sure?" I felt hot tears queuing up in my eyes.

"Sure I'm sure. Now git your fanny out of this vanny and go home to your manny!"

Hesitant at first, I opened the passenger side door and stepped out. I wasn't used to asking for, or calling in favors. I turned back for a moment with every intention of protesting, but instead I heard myself thanking her.

Sue Jan pulled the door closed and gave me the thumbs up.

While I fiddled with my key in the lock, my husband opened the door and planted a long suction-y kiss on my lips. Heaven!

"Hudson!"

"Lovita." He wrapped his arms around me, or tried. It's hard to wrap your arms around a pregnant woman without extenders, like those seatbelts on an airplane.

I heard a tiny whimper down by our feet and looked down. "Buttercup!"

Hudson reached down to pick our beloved Yorkie up and set her in the crook of my arm. Two pink bows adorned her tiny ears. Hudson must have had our sweet pup groomed. I kissed her little head. "And how are you, little darling?"

"I don't know about Buttercup, but *I* missed you." Hudson winked. He patted my belly. "And our little one."

"Silly rabbit!" I kissed his cheek.

Hudson studied my face. "You've been crying."

On the verge of more tears, I tried to nod. He hugged me again, our pup nudged cozily in between us.

"That poor woman. At least she died quickly. Do you and Sue Jan believe she died from natural causes or something else?"

"We don't know. She drank some tea, ate some cookies, and was a smoker too. There are lots of ways to poison a person."

"You'll find out soon enough. Now c'mon." He walked me inside and led me straight to the couch. "Put your feet up." He swung my feet up, removed my shoes, and tucked a pillow underneath.

"Wow, I could get used to this." I let out a huge sigh. Buttercup snuggled in the crook of my arm.

Hudson kissed my forehead and tucked a small pillow against my back. "I hope you do."

A dinger went off in the kitchen and he trotted off after it. "What's going on?" I tried to swivel from my comfortable position, but decided against it.

He hollered back. "Dinner's done. I'm bringing you a tray. Flip the TV on, will you? The news might mention my case. There were a few reporters trailing us."

"Okay." I clicked the remote and turned up the volume. And just as Hudson returned with the tray, a picture popped up on the screen of my husband and his client. "Look!"

We listened, but the report didn't offer much about the case. But I was over the moon. I hooted out, "My handsome husband made the news!"

Hudson grinned as he leaned down and slipped a napkin under my chin. "About fifteen seconds worth at least."

I sniffed. "What have we here?"

"Your favorite. King Ranch chicken. Not from scratch though. I cheated and bought a roasted chicken on the way home. Hope you like it."

I dipped a finger into the sauce and tasted. "Umm. Are you kidding me? It's delicious!"

"Let's say grace." He took my hand. But just as he did, another report caught our attention. About a Sasquatch. In Wachita. A graphic of an artist's rendition of a big mean apelike creature popped up.

"Big news." Tiffi Purewhite, the Bentley newscaster winked. "Or rather, *Bigfoot* news for the town of Wachita. Next week a television crew will follow a team of amateur investigators led by Mr. Pinkie Mountebank, President and Founder of the Society of Bigfoot Documentation and Truth Seekers, as they search for proof for the elusive creature's existence." She turned to her co-anchor. "Bob, can you believe this is happening so close to our town? And why would a Bigfoot want to live in the town of Wachita of all places?"

He scrunched his shoulders and laughed. "You got me, Tiffi."

"Bob, do you believe Bigfoot creatures are real?"

He guffawed and looked straight into the camera. "My wife sure does—whenever I take off my shoes."

"Oh Bob . . ." Tiffi attempted to snicker through the Botox, and turned to the camera. "That's it for Channel 14 news today. Tune in tonight at ten."

I sat straight up. "Oh no—Monroe is gonna be beside himself. How did they find out?"

"Beside himself, Lovita? More like gobsmacked. Word gets around fast when someone says they've seen a nine-foot-tall apelike creature. The advance people from the show are probably already in town scouting locations and all that. Those shows are all staged, you know."

"Are they really?" I took a big creamy-cheesy bite of my King Ranch chicken and passed a tiny bit to Buttercup to sample as well. "So good. Sooooo good."

"Thanks. And as to whether or not those shows are staged, you're about to become a first-hand witness."

"The detective in me welcomes the opportunity. This is the biggest mystery we've ever had in this little town, and Sue Jan and I are right in the middle of a multiple murder mystery." After I gave him a quick rundown on what was going on, I patted the sofa. "Sit down next to me and have your dinner, honey. You must be starving."

"Don't mind if I do." He pulled an easy chair close to the sofa and balanced his plate on one knee.

I took a deep breath. "Hudson, do you think? I mean, we're safe right? Is there? Could there be?"

He smiled. "A monster in the woods around Wachita? If there is, he's done a pretty good job of avoiding humans all these years. Plus, if you watch those shows, they never actually find a Bigfoot on any of the episodes, and there's a very good reason why."

"Why?" I asked.

"Because they don't exist."

"But I think they do." I held up my fork. "The Bigfoot exists in people's minds until we can prove otherwise. And I intend to do just that. Not just me. I mean, Sue Jan and I. She doesn't know it yet. We're still in the middle of the circus psycho killer thing, or whatever's going on. But the Bigfoot mystery has to be solved. For sure."

A furrow appeared on his forehead and Hudson squeezed my hand. "Lovita, I mean this in the most caring way, but please don't exert yourself too much. For the sake of our baby, please. I'm not trying to get you to quit your investigation or stop you from being a forensic female, I just want you and the baby to be okay."

A twinge of guilt hit me. I knew what he said was true. I'd been pushing myself more and more lately and feeling tired all the time. There was no way I'd do anything to jeopardize our little one. I knew I had to reassure my husband of that. "When I start getting tired and have to hang back from the footwork, I promise to stay at the salon or home. Hudson, you've got to believe me. I want the best for our baby."

He caressed my face. "Thank you Lovita. I know you do, and so do I."

"When the time comes, if I have to be an armchair detective for the remainder of my pregnancy, so be it. But I'm still going find a way to investigate."

"I know you will, because I know you too well." Hudson smiled. "Are you ready for dessert?"

I bit my lip as I fought the urge to say yes. "I think I'll pass on dessert today, honey."

His eyes flashed concern and he immediately checked my forehead for fever.

## WEIGHTY MATTERS

I moved his hand away. "I'm not sick. I just think it's a good idea to eat healthier. Don't get me wrong. I love desserts. But I decided I'm going to enjoy them now and then instead of now." I laughed. "Maybe I'll save my dessert and use it as bait to catch the Bigfoot."

The phone rang. Hudson and I stared at one another. He answered and handed the cellphone to me after he heard the voice. "It's Sue Jan."

I put her on speakerphone, but before I could tell her she was on speakerphone, Sue Jan screeched. "Ita, we're ruined! Did you hear how they dissed Wachita on the Bentley news? 'Why would a Bigfoot want to be in Wachita?'" She snorted. "How could they say something so mean about our hometown? Who wouldn't want to live here in Wachita? It's a nice little place with good values. Why, a Bigfoot would love it here. Our woods would be real comfortable for him and his hairy wife and Bigfoot babies and kin. And now them TV folks from the Bigfoot show and the news show people are here, right here, waiting outside our front door to catch Monroe and me for an interview. But Monroe don't want to talk to them yet until tomorrow. He needs time to get his story straight about what he wants to say. Could you please put Hudson on?"

"Sure, I can. And—and don't you worry. Somehow, some way, things are going to work out okay for our little town. We need to investigate this Bigfoot nonsense ASAP!"

"You bet we do, Lovita. And when I find out who's messing with us, I'm gonna kick their heiny from here to next week."

"Suey," I paused, "Bear with me for a second. For the sake of exploring all possibilities, what if there are real live Bigfoots in the world, maybe right here where we live?"

I heard a long deep audible breath on the other end of the phone.

"I don't know whether to laugh or cry at what you just said.

Face it, Lovita. If there is a real Bigfoot the only part of me he's going to see is my rear end running the other way. Here's Monroe. He's itching to talk to Hudson."

I handed the phone to Hudson and rested my head back on the couch pillow. If the circus wasn't already in town, I'd say Wachita was right in the middle of one. And the mystery of it all was big, bigger than any Sasquatch. How in the town's hundred-year-old history, had I never heard word of any Bigfoot sightings? And just as a shady circus comes to town, BINGO, a hairy creature shows up in the woods. Could the two events be somehow connected? I made up my mind to find out.

Somewhere between a psycho circus killer and a scary Sasquatch was a secret slicker than cut okra.

# CHAPTER SEVEN

■■■■■■■■■■■■■■■■■■■■■■■■■

## Trapeze Please!

"What's her name again?" I squeezed my head between my hands, hoping her name would pop out. "Why can't I remember?"

"Her name's Dixie. Now Lovita, don't worry about all the brain cells you lost being pregnant. Trust me, you'll never miss 'em."

I stuck my tongue out at her, Sue Jan style. "Gee thanks. That made me feel so much better. My brain definitely doesn't work like it used to. This is so weird."

She eyed me like she hadn't heard a word I said. "Are you feeling up to interviewing this woman? How are you doing today, by the way? I need to find out how you're doing before we go any further 'cause I promised . . ."

She stopped in her word tracks, immediately aware, according to the expression I read on her face, that she'd revealed a piece of information she shouldn't have.

"Soooo, Suey, my husband made you promise to keep an eye on me, right?"

"Ummm," Sue Jan's kewpie-doll eyes rattled from side to

side like they were looking for a way to escape her head. "He might have asked me to look after you a bit. That's okay though. I—I mean, I'm your *best* friend and all, and your husband only wants the *best* for you."

I folded my arms. "I'm fine, except for my aching feet. And I'm tired all the time. And apparently I can't remember anything anymore. On top of all that, my husband treats me like a china teacup."

"Girl, husbands do that sort of thing. They worry about their pregnant wives overdoing it and such, but our husbands have it much worse. They have to worry about us forensic females chasing crazy criminals and getting into dangerous situations."

I had to agree with Suey. But I didn't want to. The thought of being sidelined brought my blood up to a full boil.

We arrived at the main tent. A small sign announced a performance practice session. Sue Jan pulled back the tent flap to the main tent. "Yoo-hoo? Yoo-hoo? Anybody in here?"

The smell of sawdust and peanut shells hit my nostrils right away, somehow stimulating my appetite. Not that sawdust or peanut shells sounded appetizing, but I guess the circus-y smells triggered my taste buds.

Sue Jan elbowed me out of my food trance and pointed up. Dixie was swinging, literally swinging from a metal bar above us. I was relieved to see a safety net below her, but the thought of swinging around in the air Tarzan-style kind of made me sick. So I brought my eyes back down to my surroundings. And that's when I noticed the clown.

This time I elbowed Sue Jan. Somehow she combo'd a double take and a gulp at the sight of him or her or *It*. "Lovita, my Clownaphobia's about to flare up!"

"Calm down Suey. We were bound to run into one or two of 'em. We're at the circus, for goodness sake."

The clown stared back at us, a thick red grease-painted smile on his face, and a stupid daisy sticking out the top of his ridiculous hat. I did a polite kind of half-wave, a greeting that said, *I see you Mister Clown, but stay where you are. Don't come near.*

The clown was holding a rope attached to the metal bar Dixie the trapeze artist was swinging from. I guess the clown was spotting her like a gymnast. And I recalled what Gerline said, everybody knew how to do every job in the circus. I wondered what the clown would look like walking a tightrope.

When we looked back, Dixie let go of the metal bar and fell flat onto the net, bouncing expertly up and down a few times before grabbing the net with both hands and flipping over the side to her ballet-slippered-feet.

A thin muscular woman, she walked towards us, nodding to the clown who released the rope and promptly disappeared behind another tent flap.

"Hello there, ladies." She squinted. "I heard about you two." She pointed to Sue Jan. "You're the one who brought us some bad luck."

When she pointed, I noticed that her little finger had a hitch in it like it had been broken at one point. I almost laughed while wondering what the odds of a trapeze artist breaking a bone were.

Sue Jan gulped. "Well, well, we don't believe in that sort of thing. Bad luck, I mean. I wouldn't have done it on purpose though if I knew ahead of time. Out of respect."

Dixie dabbed at the back of her neck with a hand towel. "You don't believe in bad luck? If Risa were still alive, she might have a different opinion on the matter."

"Risa?" I interrupted.

"Madame Curio was her stage name. Risa's her—I mean *was* her real name."

"Oh." I nodded. "But you can't be saying what I think you're saying. That we're responsible for her death?"

She sniffed. "Not directly. I know Risa wasn't eating tofu and doing Pilates." Dixie spat into the sawdust. "But you didn't help things none."

"We're sorry about what happened." I wanted, needed her to know that. Sue Jan and I felt terrible about Madame Curio's passing.

Dixie slung the towel over a tent rope. "She was a good person and she was my friend, that's all."

The three of us were silent a moment before Sue Jan glanced around and spoke up. "Where's your partner? I mean, who catches you?"

Dixie frowned. "Lex was my partner and he quit last month. He has to pay child support and our checks weren't coming on time like they used to. Until I find someone else, it's just little old me."

I perked up at that little piece of information about paychecks being late. That suggested money problems, and money troubles provided the motive we were looking for. However, Sue Jan was headed in a different direction.

"Who's gonna catch you, Dixie?"

The woman's mouth fell open. "No one, I guess. At least, not for now. I only do routines that can be done alone. And that ain't much."

"But isn't that kind of dangerous? I mean, you're up in the air and stuff. A partner is kind of a safety net too, right?

She wagged her index finger at Sue Jan. "You're smarter than you look."

I shot a glance to Sue Jan.

"Thanks, I think."

"I'm not going to lie. Doing this alone is dangerous. That's why JoJo works the ropes while I'm on the fly bar doing sweeps. What else can I do? It's not like any Chuck off the truck can do this kind of work. Might take me a while to find someone."

Sue Jan rolled her eyes. "So in the meantime, you got a clown as a partner?"

"Uh, yeah." Dixie retrieved the towel and wiped her forehead. "If you put it like that, it doesn't sound too cool, but he lost his partner and I lost mine. I dressed up like a clown and drove a clown car to help him out in the town parade. Funny, I don't even know him that well. He only takes his greasepaint off after he turns in for the night. Pickles probably knew him better than anyone else." She glanced toward the entrance to the tent. "Is that all? Tonight is opening night and I have lots to do."

"Just a few more questions, please and we'll get out of your way," I spoke fast.

"Did Trystan have any enemies that you knew of?" Or for that matter, Johnny or Risa or *you*?"

Dixie's face flushed as Sue Jan grasped the woman's arm. "We heard you almost died from a frayed rope."

"Enough!" Dixie looked like she was going to cry. She threw down the towel and ran out of the big tent.

Sue Jan and I watched her go. I tried to reach down to pick up the towel.

"Sheesh, she really got upset about *that* question."

"Hold on, I'll get it." Sue Jan picked the towel up and handed it to me. "Why do you want her sweaty old towel?"

"Look Suey, there's a faint impression of something stenciled on the bottom in black ink."

"What is it, Ita?" Sue Jan plunged her head over my shoulder.

"A word. It looks like a name." I turned the towel slightly for a better view.

"DeSilva?"

Sue Jan laughed. "You take de silva and I'll take de gold!"

But a connection was whirring round my head like an unbalanced load of laundry. *Kaboom. Kaboom. Kaboom.* I grabbed Sue Jan by the arms. "Silver! The last word Madame

Curio said before she—"

"Pushed up daisies?" Sue Jan stuck her tongue out the side of her mouth and dropped her head to the side like she was dead. "Right. I see where you're going with this." She paused to catch her breath. "Or maybe I don't. Ita, where are you going with this?"

"We need to look for someone with that last name. "

"DeSilva." We said it together. And Sue Jan immediately whistled.

We spun around at a sudden commotion behind us and saw the clown, standing still as a statue, watching us. The painted-on frown on his face brought chill bumps to my skin. Neither one of us had to say a word. Sue Jan and I spun on our heels and headed out the tent as fast as our pregnancy flats could carry us.

On the way to the car, Sue Jan moved her lips like she was about to do that King of France thing, only I put my index finger over her mouth before she could speak.

"Give it a rest, Suey. Give it a rest."

Back at the Crown of Glory, we caught Jolene and Charla up on the goings-on of the circus case and the Sasquatch, of course. I couldn't decide which name for the monster I liked better, Bigfoot or Sasquatch. Most everybody else seemed to like Bigfoot, including Sue Jan. Bigfoot had more of a Texas vibe to it, I guess. But I decided not to decide which name to use for the fictional or not-so-fictional creature, at least for the time being.

Anyway, I decided to eat my healthy home-packed lunch in my stockroom. I sat down on a swivel-y wooden office chair I bought at a garage sale and put my feet up on an old peach crate. As I was preparing to take the first bite of my peanut butter-banana-honey sandwich on sprouted wheat, Sue Jan cracked the door open and peered in.

"Ita, my client cancelled! I know I shouldn't be happy about that, but I am. The last time she was in she told me she wanted highlights to match her natural base color, and I told her, 'Honey, you don't have a base.' Ita, the woman's hair is completely gray underneath. What else could I say? Do you think that's why she cancelled?"

"Could be." I chuckled. "No woman wants to feel old."

She came in and closed the door behind. "We need to talk."

"We sure do." I slurped through the straw in my bottle of carrot juice.

She pulled up a wooden chair and turned a bucket upside down for her feet. "Ah, ain't this the life for a couple of pregsters?" Sue Jan pulled a kiddie juice box and a can of sardines out of a brown paper bag and peeled back the top of the tin. "Ita, I got cravings. Can you tell?"

"Gaah!" The fishy oily smell hit me and mixa-wixied with the peanut butter-banana-honey thing I had going on in my mouth. And the immediate result? I started getting green around the gills.

"What's wrong?" Sue Jan sucked in a couple of silver sardine tails as she spoke.

"I'm begging you. Unless you're a seal and I don't know it, stop eating that nasty stuff in front of me. That smell is making me sick."

"Are you serious? You gonna call for O'Rourke or something?"

"Uh, yeah . . . "

"Oh all right, Ita. Pregnancy sure makes you grouchy."

"Ugh." I held my empty plastic sandwich bag to my mouth in case I needed to use it. Somehow, just knowing the bag was there gave me comfort.

Sue Jan snatched the bag from my hand. But before she

stuffed the open tin of sardines inside and sealed it, she tipped the open sardine can to her mouth and gulped down the oily juice.

I felt my insides churn. "That's about the grossest thing I've ever seen anyone do."

She shrugged and wiped her mouth with a section of paper towel. "Done! Are you satisfied?" She eyed my lunch bag. "I'm still hungry. You got another one of them sandwiches in there?"

I handed her the bag. "You know I always make two." I waited until she took a couple of bites. "So, we need to find out some info about that man who couldn't pay his gambling debt and lost the circus."

"*An look up thath name, DeShilva, too*," Sue Jan added, through a mouthful of sandwich.

I rubbed my palms together to shake off the crumbs and then reached for my laptop. A quick Google of Mordecai's Circus revealed something interesting. "Listen up, Suey. The man who lost the circus to Trystan Whipsnade in an epic poker game was in fact, named Mordecai DeSilva. And the man didn't take the loss well at all. He vowed revenge on Trystan and his entire family. Spat and uttered a Gypsy curse, the whole nine yards."

"Well there's your man! He's got a murder motive, at least for Gerline's daddy. I'm not sure about Pickles or Madame Curio though, or the attempted murders of Johnny and Dixie and Max. Unless he wanted to get back at the entire circus! All we need to do is find him."

I snorted. "Ratty-tatty darns!"

"What is it?" Sue Jan gulped the last bite of her sandwich.

"He's missing."

"You mean there ain't no more Mordecai?"

"Well, as far as I can tell there's no proof that he's dead. Just missing."

Sue Jan stood up and looked over my shoulder at the screen. "Ita, click the third newspaper article link." She slurped through a tiny juice box straw and pointed to the image.

An old newspaper article headlined a missing person article. "Suey, it's just another article about Mordecai going missing."

"Are you sure? Keep reading, girl." She started reading out loud. "...His distraught wife, Nellia DeSilva..."

"Why does that name ring a bell?"

"Sheesh, Ita, how many brain cells has the baby sucked out of your head? Take another looksee at this photo. Recognize that face at all? It's Cornelia when she was young, without a crumpled dishrag face. The nose is what gives her away."

"Nellia? Nellia is Cornelia! Of course! So Cornelia was, or is, his wife? I guess Nellia's her nickname or something."

Sue Jan nodded. "Correcto-mundo. And their daughter Dixie sure kept her cards close when we interviewed her. I knew in my knower that woman was hiding something."

"If she's the wife she's got to know something." I exhaled loud. "Like where her husband is."

Sue Jan snorted. "Or *she* could be the one who murdered Trystan, maybe even working with her kids. And how easy would it be for that trapeze-y chimpanzee daughter of his to rig a sandbag to fall on Trystan's head? Maybe Cornelia wanted to take over the circus herself. The criminal mind is hard for us normal people to understand. Nothing rings up right at the register for those kind of folks."

"These are all just ideas." I shook my head. "We need a concrete motive. Who else could have known?"

"Madame Curio, that's who." Sue Jan pointed out. "Dixie said Risa was her friend."

"Why would she kill her best friend? You're *my* best friend and I would never think of doing something like that to you. Although there are times when I think I want to clobber you." I gave Sue Jan a cheesecake grin.

She stuck her tongue out at me. "That's the head-scratcher,

Ita. That's a crazy way to end a friendship!"

"Dixie could be fruit loops from swinging around on a trapeze her whole life or maybe she's a natural born circus psycho killer."

"Those are some interesting ideas. Or Cornelia could have done away with Risa because she knew too much and was a potential threat. One things for sure, we've got to find out more about them." I started X'ing out of the previous pages I'd visited, but stopped when my eye caught something. "Wait a minute." I swung my feet off the crate and stood. "Look at the date! Today is exactly one year from Trystan's death. The killer might try and go after someone else at the circus tonight."

Sue Jan scrunched her face. "Why Lovita? What makes you think the killer is interested in anniversaries?"

I lifted my laptop so she could get a better look. "Part of the gypsy curse in that same article. It says here that Mordecai claimed if the circus wasn't returned to him within a year's time, someone would die before the next full moon, and every year thereafter. Trystan died at the close of that first year during the full moon cycle."

"Ita, I think you're on to something." Sue Jan siphoned the last drop of juice from her kiddie juice box.

"C'mon Suey, you and I had better go have a talk with the sheriff about this. If someone is killing the ringmasters, that means Gerline could be in danger when she's filling in for Mini Maxi tonight."

# CHAPTER EIGHT

### Send In The Clowns

"Are you nervous?" Hudson put his arm around me.

"You kidding me? I'm on pins and needles. I just hope nothing bad happens."

Hudson led me from the car towards the circus grounds, following a crowd of townsfolk and a hefty amount of people I didn't recognize, probably from Bentley. I knew he was afraid I would trip on the uneven ground or something like that, but all his clucking after me in my final trimester made me feel like an invalid.

"Lovita, I can't believe the man's daughter is still going on with the show after one of her performers died under unexplained circumstances."

"Gerline?" I replied. "She told me and Sue Jan that with circus folk, the show goes on no matter what."

Hudson grimaced. "It's the 'no matter what' part that bothers me." He cast a glance over his shoulder. "Monroe told me that the sheriff and deputy are supposed to be here tonight in plainclothes so they won't attract attention."

"Really?" I looked over my shoulder and to the side but

didn't spot them. "I'm glad. It's a comfort to know they'll be keeping a close watch on things. I don't want anyone else to, you know . . ."

Calliope music fluttered its joyful cheer through the air, in sharp contrast to my dismal thoughts. And somehow at that same moment, the fragrance of fresh-popped popcorn made my mouth water. "Honey?"

Before I could say another word, he answered. "I'll be sure to get you some darling." He winked. "That carny corn smells so good I might have to buy one for myself too."

We settled into our reserved seats, in a set of bleachers Gerline called the "grandstand," the seats nearest to the rings. She'd set us up with an 'Annie Oakley', circus talk for complimentary tickets and reserved seating—Sue Jan and Monroe, me and Hudson and Jolene and Charla and their dates too, as a thank-you for helping Max. Curious, I had asked Gerline why free tickets were called Annie Oakleys and she told me they punched holes in the free ones, which made the tickets look like the playing cards the wild west sharp-shooter Annie Oakley used to shoot a hole through in her shows.

JoJo the scary clown was already working the crowd, twisting balloon animals for the kids. And a skinny Asian guy whom I quickly figured to be the Yo-Yo Master, shot out yo-yos from both sides of his body. Like a sort of yo-yo spider man, the strings launched the lollipop-sized yo-yo forward and back and to the sides and up and down. Fascinated, I watched him until my eyes started crossing. So I focused on the opposite side of the tent. I recognized Trick and the other man we'd seen on unicycles, only this time they were on unicycles and juggling as well. And they were wearing shiny satin costumes. I saw another walking around on stilts in a crazy Uncle Sam costume. And Dixie in a bejeweled, bedazzled leotard, a little on the skimpy side in my opinion, waved to the audience as she swung back and forth above the ring on her fly bar.

A couple of acrobats launched off one another's shoulders, hopping around like there were springs on their feet, and a plate twirler kept three plates on three sticks spinning round and round, which I hate to admit, kept me hypnotized for a while. Until I spotted the sword swallower, that is. Short, and to the point. *Hehe.* Zeke's pretty wife apparently swallowed swords for a living, besides the tattoo'd woman gig. And she was killing it, particularly to one section of the audience, clapping steadily nearby. Zeke was supposed to come out after her, breathing fire, of all things. The couple had mad skills. Mad, as in crazy.

Poor Johnny Roo walked back and forth, a sandwich board hanging on his drooping shoulders. The sign advertised the Sideshow tent, a special small tent outside the main Big Top, featuring intriguing items listed in bullet points, likely Gerline's business-y idea. But the man might as well have been wearing some kind of look-at-me-I'm-a-dunce cap. He couldn't have pretended to be more miserable.

I read through the sign. Some of the highlighted items in the Sideshow tent included an alien egg, two-headed snake, and a mermaid preserved in Formaldehyde. Which brought to mind those old ads in comic books for sea monkeys. I remember sending off for some and hoping I'd get to raise a sea monkey family like the ad pictured them. But I learned a hard lesson. Sea monkeys were not as advertised. Ugh.

Some of the other items featured in the Sideshow were bones from a so-called giant, and the freeze-dried body of a Chupacabra, whatever a Chupacabra was or is. But the main attraction in the tent was a supposed tuft of fur from a real live Sasquatch. A what? That last bullet point item interested me the most. I resolved to visit the Sideshow tent before we left the circus. But I had to wonder. What if all the talk about a Bigfoot in Wachita was a big fib to create interest or a buzz so people would want to visit their Sideshow Tent?

A man selling peanuts and popcorn came by and, true to his word, Hudson bought a small red-and-white striped box for each of us. He even asked the popcorn vendor for some buttery popcorn salt to add since we were used to having butter on ours.

Sue Jan and Monroe arrived at the same time as Jolene and Dr. Colley, and as soon as Sue Jan saw our snack, she had Monroe chase down the vendor.

"Hey Ita, and Hudson." Sue Jan eyed my popcorn. "I wonder what's taking Monroe so long."

I laughed, "He's been gone less than a minute."

Sue Jan pouted. "I wish we could have brought the twins with us tonight to see the show, but," she whispered, "not if something bad happens. Maybe when we solve these mysteries, I'll take them to a daytime performance."

Charla showed up alone and kind of sad-looking. She and her boyfriend Zane broke up a couple of weeks earlier, which made the situation at work kind of awkward because of Zane being Jolene's son and all. Honestly though, I felt like Jolene was okay with them breaking it off. No mama ever thinks any girl is good enough for her boy.

Suddenly a succession of spotlights flashed on and off and on and off again, signaling the show was about to begin. The performers took the cue to disappear behind the stage area. And then the lights went completely out. Hudson squeezed my hand.

The excitement building, the crowd hushed as the rhythmic beating of a snare drum announced the show was about to begin. Two spotlights flicked on and lit up the center of the ring where Gerline sat, glittery blue eye shadow glimmering from her lids. She wore a red jacket. Hair in a sleek ponytail, her black top hat angled coquettishly to the side on her head. But the most interesting accessory? She gripped a leather riding crop in both hands. Dumbstruck at her transformation, I forgot how to swallow until I heard her voice boom over a hand-held mic.

"Good evening and welcome to the Greatest Little Circus and Sideshow in the U. S. of A. The famous, the infamous, Mordecai's Circus and Sideshow! I am Ruby Rappaport, your ringmaster, and Mistress of Ceremonies at your service. Our show will awe and amaze you with phantasmagorical, fantabulous, jaw-dropping, far-flung feats and wonders. Stroll into our Sideshow and be enthralled by a bizarre and beguiling compendium of oddities and rare, forbidden, exhibits of mystic and magical creatures hidden from the known world."

Her voice faded away as the volume of my own thoughts turned up. Ruby Rappaport? Why was Gerline using a stage name? But then I remembered her real name. *Gerline Whipsnade.*

From the business end, the woman was trying to keep this bojankety circus together with nothing more than chewing gum and baling wire, but from the performance end, I had to admit, she had a certain flair for words. She knew how to work dramatic pauses to her advantage, and how to angle her face so it looked best under the lights, and she sure was a pro at batting those spiders masquerading as false eyelashes. The woman definitely how to dress for a circus performance too. But most importantly, Gerline knew how to put up some killer jazz hands when the music started playing. Music? I'd been so lost in my crazy thoughts, I'd missed the rest of her introduction.

So I was totally thrown off guard when the spotlight landed on 'The Amazing, The One and Only, Teeny Carlini.' Since the death of Madame Curio had delayed the circus opening night, Max had been released from the hospital. I wondered why Max had skipped the ringmaster part since he was so taken with the role. But then again, maybe doing the magic tricks was likely about all he could handle so soon after his hospital stay.

Like Dixie, the trapeze artist, Teeny Carlini worked without an assistant. Unlike Dixie however, if something went wrong with his act, the worst that could happen would be some booing from the audience.

In my opinion, Teeny Carlini's tricks, much like the cereal I grew up eating, were for kids. Nothing fancy. The old coin-and-card tricks. Pulling a rabbit out of his black top hat, streaming colorful scarves from his tiny sequined jacket, and pulling apart a couple of metal hoops. *Meh.* The same old magic trick shtick. I chalked it up to the fact that janky, no-frills circuses like Moredecai's made do with what they had to work with. The best magic trick the man did was his exit. Literally. Teeny Carlini made a rope stand straight up in the air and then climbed it and disappeared. That one really lassoed me in.

Dr. Colley clapped the hardest for Teeny. He leaned over to talk to Jolene. "I can't believe how good he's doing. I wanted to keep him an extra day but he insisted on performing."

"The show must go on." Jolene laughed.

Then they laughed together. And they snuggled close to each other, sealing their lips in what seemed like a never-ending kissy-kissy fest.

I felt a sour pucker forming on *my* lips and I happened to glance over at Sue Jan. Apparently she'd noticed the two of them as well. And the look on her face told me she didn't approve either. Jolene and the doctor had become *that* couple, the annoying duo that shuts out the rest of the world, the couple that shows way too much PDA, the couple that other couples want to uncouple.

"Lovita?" Hudson's voice sounded strange.

"What?"

"Look!" He pointed up above the ring at the same moment a shrill scream sounded, followed by many more from the bleachers.

A spotlight maneuvered to reveal the situation. The fly bar Dixie had been swinging on earlier was now hanging by one rope and Dixie's life, by a thread! Again? Another attempt on her life in the same way? The circus psycho killer didn't have much imagination. A harried group of performers brought out a safety net and held it beneath her. But Dixie somehow pulled herself up the rope, resting one foot on the fly bar and began swinging back and forth to gain enough momentum to land back on her precarious perch.

Sheriff Wilkes and Deputy Phelps ran from the bleachers to the ring and held the crowd back from entering. But Dixie, in a few short, tense, bloodcurdling minutes, grasped a rope at her perch and managed to climb down the ladder to the loudest applause I'd ever heard.

Hudson and I looked at one another. He wrapped an arm around me. "That was too close for comfort, Lovita."

"And too much of a coincidence." Sue Jan added, leaning in close. "But you can't trust what you see. Even salt looks like sugar, you know."

*Where was Sue Jan coming up with these little snippets of wisdom?* I was about to ask my friend what she meant by that when a sudden sick-y kind of feeling overwhelmed me. I gripped Hudson's arm. "Honey, I can't believe I'm saying this, but I think I need to leave."

"What? Are you okay?" Maybe the feeling was making my brain all wonky but my husband's eyes looked huge to me.

"I'm not sure."

Hudson tugged Dr. Colley's sleeve and he and Jolene came apart like North-to-North magnets. "Sorry to interrupt. I hope you don't mind, but Lovita's not well."

Dr. Colley shifted gear into medical mode right away. He pulled out a penlight, lifted my eyelids, looked in my throat, checked my temp, felt my pulse and, like a medical magician, pulled a stethoscope out of his collar and listened to my heart.

"It's probably the popcorn I ate. My stomach is all

catawampus."

"Your heart's beating a bit fast, Lovita. Digesting popcorn isn't easy on a system that's already stressed. Plus, all your organs are pushed out of place to make room for the baby."

"Gross." Sue Jan made a face as she munched a handful of popcorn.

"I'm just trying to tell Lovita that when you're as pregnant as she is, that things get a little crowded in—in there." He added, "I would call your OB tomorrow though, just to be safe."

"I'm going in tomorrow morning for a checkup, Dr. Colley."

Hudson shook his hand. "Lovita and I really appreciate your help." Then Hudson stood and reached for my hand. "Are you ready to go home now, honey?"

My husband helped me up and navigated me down the bleachers. As we exited the tent, I took one last longing look at the ring. Our friends waved from the Annie Oakley seats, and a wave of disappointment came over me, like Christmas had just been cancelled or something.

The new moon cast a surreal light on the temporary circus grounds as passing clouds dimmed our path. A makeshift parking lot hosted a sea of cars, muddied to greyish hues in the glow. The whole way back to the car, I felt nauseous, and angry, that I never got the chance to have a look at the curious items inside the Sideshow Tent.

"Hudson, I hope we'll be able to come back tomorrow night. I didn't get to see the rest of the acts or the other tent and I really want to."

"That depends on how you feel. If you feel up to it, of course we'll go." He wagged a finger. "But you'll have to stay away from popcorn."

"The way I feel now, popcorn's gonna have to stay away from me." Hudson's arm around my shoulders somehow made me feel better about my situation. Even though my stomach still felt weird.

"We're almost to the car, honey. When we get home, maybe you could take an antacid for your stomach."

I stopped in my tracks. "Do you smell something?" I made a hand tent and covered my nose. "Yuck!" Bile raced up and down at the back of my throat like a thermometer that couldn't make up its mind.

Hudson caught the waft and blinked. "What is that? It's positively awful." He brought his sleeve up to his nose.

And right at that moment, the clouds that had cast a shadow over our path passed along and I saw a silhouette of someone standing against the luminescent light. I panted at the sight. Not someone. *Something.*

"Hudson," I paused, shock registering. "What is THAT?" Whatever we were both gawking at was something I'd never ever seen before and would never, ever want to see again.

Hudson's voice squeaked out. "I think it's uhhhh-ahhh."

"What?"

My husband could barely move his mouth. "I-I think it's ahhhh—a Bigfoot!"

Hudson and I froze when he named the name. I had to admit, when talk of the Bigfoot came up, I wanted to believe they existed, but didn't really believe in them. The detective chick in me decided that there must be some sort of explanation. But I never considered the possibility that the hairy creatures could be real.

The creature turned slightly and I got a side-glance at his snarly face. And I realized that this was not gonna be a Harry-and-the-Hendersons moment. The thing was big, as in nine feet, I guessed. Hairy, as in brownish-reddish hair all over its body. The face kind of reminded me of a gorilla, but different. More human looking. And he definitely did not have a pleasant expression on his chops.

Chill bumps ran up and down my arms and spine and the back of my head like I'd just accidentally eaten a glob of wasabi, which actually did happen to me once.

Voice shaking, I whispered. "Hudson, are we really seeing what I think we're seeing?"

"I—I—I" was all my husband could manage to say.

For a man who worked in the absolutes, seeing a big hairy monster wasn't setting well with him. And it wasn't setting well with me either. My mouth locked into an "O" shape.

Finally the creature uttered a loud cry like a war whoop. Then it leapt up on the hood of a beat-up white Ford Ranger and spring-boarded off into the woods.

My first instinct was to scream, then run, then run screaming back to the circus to fetch the sheriff and deputy and bring them back to see what we saw, but the baby in my tummy and the bile in my throat had other ideas. So I decided to kill two birds with one stone and go with running away from the big scary monster while I yodeled my groceries.

# CHAPTER NINE

■■■■■■■■■■■■■■■■■■■■■■■■■

## Get Into The Act

Getting that rancid popcorn out of my system turned out to be the cure for what ailed me, and apparently for Hudson too. My grocery yodeling triggered him as well. Neither of us had ever thrown up on the run before. Come to think of it, this was the first time I'd ever seen Hudson sick at all. I guess it's like my mama always said, 'There's a first time for everything.' Anywho, by the time we made it back to the circus tent, my husband and I both felt better. Weak in the knees, and terrified, but better.

We found Monroe first and after we told him what happened, I thought his wire-rimmed glasses were gonna crack. I nudged Sue Jan. "He's white as a marshmallow."

Sue Jan tee-hee'd. "I had a dream I was eating a marshmallow one night. When I woke up, my pillow was missing."

I rolled my eyes. "Suey, now is not the time for jokes. Your husband's really upset. Do something."

She reached over and thumped her husband's cheeks. "Honey, snap out of it! If Lovita and Hudson said they saw a Bigfoot, then they really did see a Bigfoot. What are you gonna do about it?" She turned to me.

"Ita, I wish I'd seen one. From a distance, that is. You said they smell real bad?"

Sue Jan was so loud she started attracting attention. People on our perimeter were listening in on the conversation. Though to be fair, I guess anyone's ears would perk up if somebody said they spotted a Bigfoot in the area.

Hudson looked Monroe in the eyes. "Friend, you know I'm not given to fantasies. I wouldn't automatically assume that a beast like this would or could exist, but I must admit, Lovita and I saw something very strange. Something we can't explain. And to tell the truth, we're both pretty shook up about it. I need to get my wife home. I want her to be safe."

"I believe you." Monroe looked from Hudson to me. "Both of you." He gulped.

Monroe brought the sheriff and deputy over. After we explained to the lawmen what had happened, I noticed Sheriff Wilkes and Deputy Phelps exchange a look like we were all cray cray. But Monroe pulled the mayor card and made them take us serious. He reminded them about the investigators coming to town and all the stuff local hunters were reporting.

So I suggested they follow us back to the scene of the sighting. And of course Sue Jan and Monroe and Dr. Colley and Jolene and Charla came along too.

They lit up the area with heavy-duty LED police flashlights. But I knew they wouldn't spot a Bigfoot. That fellow was long gone. Once he leapt off that truck and . . .

"That's it!" I yelled.

"Where?" Wilkes and Phelps ran around in circles.

"No, I—I just remembered. That thing jumped up on a truck." I pointed in the direction. And the two lawmen followed my index finger with their flashlights to the direction of the Ford Ranger.

Just then, a herd of clouds darkened the view, but the LED lights settled on the milky white of the truck, reflecting off the headlights. By the time we made it to the vehicle, the clouds cleared off and the moonlight illuminated the scene.

"Take a look at that." Sheriff Wilkes gestured to his deputy. The expression on his face was a lot different. The hood of the truck had a deep indent and marks that looked like muddy footprints. They examined the ground around the truck too.

"Bazooka." Deputy Phelps looked down.

The deputy was busy taking down our statements while the sheriff measured and took pictures. Then I heard a commotion and looked behind us, realizing to my horror there was a small crowd of people gathering. I plucked on Hudson's sleeve and pointed behind us. By then, a couple of men with over-the-shoulder film cameras were approaching. Likely the advance team for that Sasquatch show. Good grief.

Monroe called out to the sheriff. "People are going to be leaving the circus in another fifteen or twenty minutes. How are you going to keep them from getting to their cars?"

Hudson whispered in Monroe's ear and he spun around, eyes wide with horror. For Monroe, the only thing worse than seeing a Sasquatch was seeing a Sasquatch film crew in his town.

The sheriff answered, "You let us worry about that Mayor. That's what you pay us for. We're going to cordon off the area around the truck and the truck itself for now."

With that said, Sheriff Wilkes pulled out a roll of yellow crime-scene tape and announced, "This here is the scene of an investigation. You folks can't go traipsing all over it. I want everyone to back up ten yards from this tape."

"Okay, I guess." Monroe's voice sounded hollow. Maybe because his voice was so low, the sheriff didn't hear his response. Monroe squinted at Hudson. "Did the way the sheriff answered me sound sort of disrespectful?"

Hudson shook his head. "Don't read too much into it. They're probably just rattled by what they found. Believe me, I'm still rattled." Hudson turned to me. "Aren't you, honey?"

I was about to tell him I felt pretty good considering all that happened, though my stomach was starting to growl. But I didn't want to make my husband feel like a wimp. "I think we should head home now if we can get out of this parking lot. We need to catch our breath."

Thankfully, our vehicles were parked away from the truck, so we decided to leave. Monroe wanted to stay and keep an eye on the investigation, so we offered to give Sue Jan a lift home. Charla asked for a ride too.

I adjusted the satellite radio in the car to a fifties station. We all needed something cheerful to listen to.

"Thanks for giving me a ride tonight Miz Lovita, and Mister Hudson. I couldn't face being in the car with them lovey-doveys no more. Plus, it feels kind of weird being that close to Jolene after me and Zane broke up. I love Miz Jolene, but my feelings for Zane are different now."

I rested my arm over the seat and examined her face. "Do you mind if I ask why?"

Charla squinted back tears. "Zane's turned into a sofa spud. He don't believe in working no more. He plays video games all day and goes after get-rich-quick schemes. Hard work ain't part of his plan to be successful."

"I thought he changed, you know, straightened up?" Sue Jan's brows arched.

"I thought he did too. Zane was doing real good for a while cheffing in that barbecue restaurant and then with that food booth in town, until he started gambling online and playing video games. Then he flat-out stopped cooking and cheffing and working hard and dreaming big. But the last straw was when he asked me to draw out all my savings to invest in one of his schemes. I work hard and save hard for a better future. I have dreams. And dreams don't come true behind bars."

"What?" Sue Jan's eyes flashed. "He asked you what?"

Charla continued. "He asked me for all my hard-earned money. That's when I knew it was over. Zane just wants a girl with a real job to pay the bills like his momma always did for him." She folded her arms. "And asking me to get involved in one of his shady schemes is just plain disrespectful."

"Does Jolene know he's involved in stuff like that?" I questioned.

She shook her head. "I doubt it. He plays the good son with her. She don't know what he's up to. Besides," she giggled, "Jolene's too busy playing tonsil hockey with the good doctor all the time."

Sue Jan stuck two fingers near her mouth like she was either going to laugh or vomit. "I hear ya, girl. Too much is too much. I'm not a fan of public displays of infection except for holding hands and a quick peck on the cheek."

I twisted my lip when I heard what she said. "Ah, Sue Jan, the word is *affection*, not *infection*. But I totally agree about PDA. Drives me bananas."

"You can add me to that roster too," Hudson called from the driver's seat.

I smiled at my husband and, in a twist of irony, felt the urge to kiss him for saying that.

Sue Jan continued. "I'll bet if Dr. Colley and Jolene had been walking to their car instead of Lovita and Hudson, they wouldn't have seen a Bigfoot, unless he looked like a big tongue, that is. Nope, they would have missed him."

"Oh Suey!" I laughed. "Yuck."

Charla bent over laughing. And I noticed Hudson chuckling as well.

I reached over and held Charla's hand. "I'm sorry about your breakup. I—I know you and Zane were in love at one time. Seems like he's going back to his old ways instead of continuing to move forward."

Tears pooled in her beautiful blue eyes. "Miz Lovita, I can't go backwards. I'm trying to get out of the trailer park, not move back in."

"And you're doing good, girl." Sue Jan grinned. "Charla, you're my kin and I'm so proud of you I could spit out blue ribbons! You are a success story if I ever heard one, what with your natural smarts and your hairstyling career at the Crown of Glory and your long-term dream of owning your own salon someday. Plus that, your family's making money managing Swain's old pig farm and living in a real house on some land instead of living in a broke-down old trailer in a bo-jankety trailer park."

Charla leaned over to hug Sue Jan. "I know I have come a long way and I'm thankful to both you and Miz Lovita for helping me. And I'm grateful to God too. My dreams are truly coming true. But love is important, ain't it? I really thought I was in love with this man . . . "

I patted her hand. "Whatever happens, I know the right one is out there." I winked. "My advice is to take your time and concentrate on your career right now. Don't settle for Mr. Okay." I glanced over at my husband. "Mr. Right is worth waiting for."

We dropped Charla off first at the pig farm and DeWayne, Sue Jan's cousin, came out to the car as she exited. He rested his arms on my passenger window and peered in. "How are you folks. Ooh-weee, Lovita." He focused on my bulging belly. "You got one coming fresh, ain't ya?"

Hudson's right eye twitched. "That's right DeWayne, won't be long now."

"Hi," Sue Jan raised a limp hand, greeting him with a less-than-enthusiastic tone to her voice.

"Howdy cuz!" He flashed a checkerboard of missing teeth her way. DeWayne leaned in a bit more, the distinct odor of pigs emanating from his bib overalls, combined with the tainted pig farm atmosphere.

I tried breathing through my nose, but it didn't help, Eau d'piggy overwhelming and downright trumping every other smell in the vicinity. No wonder Charla was keen to make enough money to strike out on her own. Waking up every morning and shutting your eyes at night to the tune and odor of oinks wouldn't sit well with anyone. Except for DeWayne, who seemed right in his element.

"I thought I'd grab you folks by the back of your collar whilst you was here 'cause I got something to tell ya." DeWayne's eyes settled on Hudson. "I don't wanna skeer any of ya'll, but my boys and I been seeing Squatchy signs in the area. Now I know we ain't lived here in Wachita a year, but we know the woods around it pretty nice. The first couple of times we seen things we couldn't explain, it was easy to blame on being tired, but yesterday none of us was tired and we come across this."

He pulled a patch of reddish-brown fur from his shirt pocket and held it up. "This here's genu-wine Squatch hair we found stuck on a bush." He thrust it under my nose. "Smell it. Don't it smell bad? That's the odor these things put out."

I wondered how DeWayne or anyone else in the family could differentiate between smells. Living on a pig farm had to be one big Spamfest of scents. "Did you, ah, see one?" I asked. The bile was already doing the thermometer thing in my throat again. One more bad whiff would likely to put me over the edge.

He wiped the back of his neck with a soiled bandana. "Nope, we ain't seen one in the flesh, or fur, *hehe*, but we smelled 'em for sure and seen some Squatchy scat, and a lot of broken tree branches and some footprints too. And we heard some tree knocks too."

"Tree knocks? What are those?" I asked.

"Them's sounds the big fellers make. They pound on trees with their fists or a rock. Maybe even their heads for all I know. All's I know is that's how them ape fellers tell each other what's goin' on in the woods. But take a look at this here video on my phone of another fella who did see one. I interviewed him. Look, listen and learn." He pressed the play button and we watched. And I don't remember taking a breath the whole time it ran.

DeWayne asked the man, "Bubba, how'd you get that streak of white hair in the middle of your forehead?"

"Cause of what I seen."

"What you seen Bubba?"

"I was out hunting, just a-walking along through the south meadow at dusk. And that's when I spotted it."

"What?"

"A big hairy monster. He was about nine foot tall, if I'm a true blue Texan. Hairy and—and smelly. The wind was just right and this smell was coming right at me. I heard about how Squatches are supposed to stink, but I had no idea until my nose tried to leap right off my face. That thing stunk like a mattress in a flophouse."

"What happened next?" DeWayned asked.

"I seen him and he seen me and the next thing I know, that hairy beast let out an unholy howl, the likes of which I have never heard in all my fifty-seven years on this here earth."

"What'd did you do?"

"I turned and run faster than a rat up a drainpipe. Dropped my gun and almost dropped my pants along the way. I tell you, I run for my life!"

"You're here talking to me so I know you made it back to

your car. Was that thing chasing you?"

He shook his head. "No, thank the good Lord. But I was shook up, that's for sure."

Sue Jan tapped my shoulder. "What's a flophouse?"

"A cheap place to sleep for people down on their luck, I think."

"Oh, no wonder the mattresses smell bad."

"Well, what do you think of that? I don't know about you, but that chills me to the bone." DeWayne scratched at a greasy lock of hair on top of his head.

Hudson, ever the gentleman, reached over to grasp the fur. "May I?"

DeWayne turned it over to him and Hudson examined the tuft of fur under the car's interior light. "Would you, do you think you would mind if I took this piece of evidence and showed it to Monroe?"

Sue Jan's cousin stuck his thumbs in his streaky overalls and glanced back towards the house. "Man-to-man, you know I wouldn't mind letting you take that sample with you, Mister Taylor, but that there sample is pure gold to all them Sasquatch folks out there. Why, I could fetch a pretty penny for it from some big city science man. You gotta give me some surety for it. Like that there watch on your wrist. Looks like it's worth a few bucks and you'd miss it. I'd sure miss my proof that Squatches exist. That's the money, right there."

Hudson sighed and started to remove his watch, when Sue Jan hollered out her disapproval. "DeWayne. DeWayne. DeWayne. How could you repay us that way? What with all we've done for you and your kin, setting you up in a house instead of that broke-down trailer you rode into town with? And training your daughter in the beauty arts? Not to mention all the other ways we've helped you out." Nostrils flaring, she pointed her index finger at Hudson. "Keep that on." Then she turned it on DeWayne, whose eyes by this time looked like eight balls. "And you, hand over that sample. Ain't my word good enough? You'll get it back or my name ain't Sue Jan Pritchard Madson!"

DeWayne leaned into the window again and gulped. "When you put it that way, how can a man fuss? Okee dokee." He dropped the stinky fur into Sue Jan's outstretched palm.

Hudson waved. "Thanks, we'll be seeing you soon."

Before he backed away from the window, DeWayne shifted his eyes like he was looking at some kind of danger over his shoulder. "A word of warning. Be careful out there. There's some dangerous critters afoot."

With that, we sped off, and I couldn't help wondering if what DeWayne said was true. I was going to leave my window open a crack to help get rid of the smell of that 'Squatchy' fur, but the whole 'dangerous critter' thing had me wondering. What if Bigfoot creatures really did exist in Wachita? Our little town would suddenly be on the map and on the radar of the state of Texas, the entire U.S. of A. Not to mention the whole world. And our wonderful way of life would be forever changed.

# CHAPTER TEN

## Carney Blarney

After visiting my OB in the a.m. I went straight to work, hoping against hope I'd have a chance to unpack a few boxes of new merchandise for the boutique. But as soon as I walked in the busy salon, a walk-in customer plonked herself down in my chair.

An older woman with thinning hair, she had the remnants of three or four different hair colors melted rainbow-pop-style from crown to roots. She pressed something to my hand. "I brought in a picture of my ideal hairstyle. Do you think you could make my hair look like that?"

I stared at the photo and melted inside. Clients were always bringing in pictures of their dream Do's, but usually without the type of hair they needed to achieve the style. A quick exam of the picture made me smile. "I'll try my best to make this one work on you. If it's good enough for Ava Gabor, it's good enough for my customer."

"Listen up." Jolene sprinted from her station to the remote at the front desk, held it up, and turned up the volume on our salon TV.

I looked up at the screen. Tiffi Purewhite must have been

covering the circus performance the night before, though I don't know how we missed seeing her. I'm guessing the woman was patting herself on the back right about now though, because she came across the scoop of a lifetime. For a Bentley reporter, anyway. The scoop—a Bigfoot sighting in the makeshift circus parking area.

I got a good look at poor Monroe on camera, sweaty forehead and all. Tiffi stood before him, a stern look on her face. The small crowd that had followed us must have overheard what was going on. And Tiffi Purewhite with her perfect plastic surgeon-y upturned nose had sniffed out the story:

"I'm standing here with the Mayor of Wachita, Monroe Madson. Now tell us, Mayor Madson, are the rumors we're hearing true? Was there in fact a Bigfoot sighting here on the circus grounds tonight in the city of Wachita?

The mayor gulped so hard I thought he'd swallowed his tongue. "Y-yes, there was a reported sighting tonight and the sheriff is—is investigating the incident."

Tiffi thrust the mic closer to Monroe's face. "Yes, we see the yellow tape cordoning off the area. Can you tell us what exactly happened?"

Obviously caught off guard in front of the camera, Monroe didn't come across too well. Sweating profusely, Monroe looked like he was fixin' to pass out. I couldn't bear to watch any more.

But even as I turned away from the newscast, I heard a commotion and glanced out the picture window. A news van? Parked right out in front of the Crown of Glory.

Sue Jan saw it too and snapped into action. "Quick, Lovita, duck into the stockroom!"

Without even thinking, I obeyed her command. But if I had taken a few more seconds to think about it, I would have said, "Why? I could answer a few questions about the situation." Like, if Tiffi asked me whether or not I'd ever set eyes on a Bigfoot, I could answer that just fine. "You're darn tooting I seen one. And he was big, really big to the tune of nine-foot-tall kinda big. I'd swear it on a stack of Bibles. Yessirree."

Instead I could hear Sue Jan chattering away in front of the camera. And suddenly it occurred to me, Sue Jan wanted her share of the limelight. A ham at heart, I should have known she'd be desperate for a little attention. I opened the stockroom door a crack further so I could see *and* hear what was going on.

"Well, Miz Purewhite or Tiffi. Can I call you Tiffi?" Sue Jan giggled. "I love that name so much. Maybe I'll name my baby that if it's a girl."

"I suppose so." Tiffi shot an annoyed look to her cameraman, motioning him to lower the camera. Apparently Tiffi wasn't interested in filming yet.

"My best friend, Lovita . . . "

Tiff pulled out a small electronic tablet and began pecking out letters. "Her full name please."

"Oh," Sue Jan's voice lowered a bit, "sure. Her name is Lovita Mae Horton Taylor, and she's married to Hudson Taylor."

"The hunky attorney?" Tiffi's face lit up as she typed.

Sue Jan paused. "Why yes, that's him. And—and they're expecting their first little baby soon."

"Oh." Tiffi pecked out the information without a lick of enthusiasm.

I pushed open the stockroom door and emerged, managing a surprised look on my face, at least I hoped that's what it looked like to everyone. "Sue Jan, I—"

Tiffi's mouth opened wide.

"What's going on?" I looked from Tiffi to Sue Jan. "I was in the stockroom." I figured I would just state the obvious, which was true. I just left off the part about hiding. No way was I gonna lie that I was working back there.

"Mrs. Taylor?" Tiffi shook my hand. "Good to meet you. I

was hoping I would." She cast a sideways glance at Sue Jan. "Mrs. Madson was about to tell me about your strange experience last night on the circus grounds. Would you mind? I'd prefer to hear a first-hand account." She motioned to the cameraman to start rolling.

She pressed her lips together to freshen her lipstick and stared straight at the camera.

"We're at the Crown of Glory Beauty Salon in Wachita where Lovita Taylor is employed as a hairdresser."

Sue Jan bellowed. "She owns the salon and boutique, along with me."

Tiffi kept her cool and continued.

"Owner and Operator Lovita Taylor—"

"We're partners." Sue Jan interrupted again. "If you're gonna report on stuff you gotta get it right, Tiff."

The reporter made a motion to cut and as soon as the camera stopped shooting, Eyes blazing, Tiffi turned to Sue Jan. "That's Miss Purewhite." She pointed her mic at Sue Jan. "And you need to stop interrupting me. It's a good thing this isn't a live broadcast."

Sue Jan drew closer to the woman and lowered her voice. "It's kind of important for you to say that Lovita and I are partners, not employees. We're business owners here in Wachita, and I happen to be the mayor's wife."

"Also," I spoke up, "If you don't mind, it's the Crown of Glory Beauty Salon and Boutique. We sell boutique items here."

"All right already." Tiffi flipped her blonde do to the side. "Can we continue?"

"Sure, sure." I nodded to her and to Sue Jan.

The cameraman hoisted the camera back onto his shoulder.

"Tiffi Purewhite here at the Crown of Glory Beauty Salon and Boutique and I'm standing with the two co-owner/operators of that salon, Lovita Taylor and Sue Jan Madson." She held the mic out to me. "Now Lovita, your business partner was telling me earlier that you had some sort of encounter with a mysterious figure on the circus grounds last night. Could you elaborate?"

"I—I'll try. My husband and I are still pretty shook up about it."

Tiffi nodded, her eyes registering empathy.

"We were on our way to our car. I wasn't feeling good after eating the circus popcorn. A doctor friend told me it was probably a pregnancy thing, but my husband felt sick too." I stared into Tiffi's eyes and somehow the woman was telling me to get on with it. "Anyway, there was a full moon, but the clouds were moving fast and when some clouds moved out of the way and the moonlight lit things up, that's when we saw it."

"Saw what?" she asked me.

"It—it was a creature of some sort. Big, maybe nine feet tall and hairy."

"A creature? Do you mean, a Bigfoot? Also known as a Sasquatch or Yeti?"

I gulped. "If any of those names are what you want to call it, then yes. My husband and I saw the creature and it jumped up on top of a pickup truck and launched off into the woods."

"What did you do after that?"

Sue Jan pulled the mic toward her. "She and Hudson ran for their lives back to the circus tent where they found us."

Tiffi pulled the mic back and stared straight at the red light over the camera.

"There you have it—a live Sasquatch sighting in the town of Wachita. My research has unearthed this exclusive report about a series of disturbing sightings by hunters and hikers in the Wachita area." She looked at Sue Jan. "I'm here with the mayor's wife, co-owner of the posh Crown of Glory Salon and Boutique. The mayor's office has denied these reports. However, if you remember, I previously reported an interesting bit of news. The advance team for the wildly popular television show featuring a team of amateur investigators lead by Mr. Pinkie Mountebank, President and Founder of the Society of Bigfoot Documentation and Truth Seekers, are in the town of Wachita, and the stars of the show, including Mr. Mountebank, are due to arrive in town today. I will be interviewing them in just a couple of hours, in time for the evening broadcast. Tune in as I said, for that exclusive interview with the stars of that show. Until then, I'm Tiffi Purewhite, your Channel 14 news investigative reporter." She lowered the mic and barked at the cameraman. "Let's get out of here. We need to set up for the evening interview."

But as she was gathering her stuff, a brilliant idea came to me. *I get one every now and then, believe it or not.* And I say 'brilliant' because the idea turned out to be just that. "Hey Miz Tiffi, since you're in our salon and all why don't you let us freshen up your hair and makeup, on the house?"

"What?" She did a turnabout.

"Have a seat right here." Sue Jan grabbed a towel and beat it against the seat to clear away any stray hairs. "We'll fix you right up."

Now I've never claimed to be a mind reader, but I could tell that the woman's thoughts were engaged in some kind of a tug-of-war. But I could tell by all the work she'd had done, that for Tiffi Purewhite, looking pretty was Priority One. She turned to the cameraman. "You and the rest of the crew, take five outside."

She sat down. "Let's get on with it."

"Sure, sure." Sue Jan winked at me. She knew exactly what I was doing. Sue Jan would do the woman's hair. We'd have Charla touch up her makeup and I would ask her questions.

Sue Jan tried to comb through the woman's spider web of Aqua-Net. "Wow, ah, you really laid it on thick."

Tiffi snapped back. "What do you expect? There's a lot of humidity forecasted for today and tomorrow."

"All the same," Sue Jan suggested, "would you mind if I gave you a quick wash and blow dry and style? I could do a better job that way."

"I don't have time."

I was quick to join the conversation. "Sue Jan can get your hair done in a flash. She's that good."

Tiffi threw up her hands. "All right. Go ahead. But please hurry."

While Sue Jan was washing the snappy woman's hair, I couldn't help noticing the condition it was in. Thin, stick-straight and dull. Styling it was gonna be a bugaboo. The woman likely took an hour or more just to tease it. I pulled Jolene, our resident tease-specialist aside. Jolene would never think of leaving her house without floofing her thin hair to high heaven. She used to sport a drab bone hair color, but then she switched to a reddish, and dare I say, more Sasquatchy color? But these days her hair was a toned-down cinnamon with lots of brownish tones blended in. She still teased it though. Teased her hair into something that resembled a tumbleweed covered with a thin layer of straight and shiny hair on the outer core. Like a Tootsie Pop. However, few people aside from the Crown of Glory staff would ever know. It's true what they say about 'only your hairdresser knows for sure.' And we do.

"Jo," I motioned with my chin, "Sue Jan's gonna need help with that. You available?"

Jolene bit her lip. "I have to ring my client up, that's all. You're right, she will need some help with *that* hair."

Sue Jan was smoothing product in Tiffi's hair and was about to commence with blow-drying. I knew the time was right, so I started asking her questions.

"You must be so excited Miz Purewhite, I mean, interviewing those guys from that show."

Tiffi rolled her eyes. "They're morons."

"You—you don't believe in what they're doing?"

"Are you kidding me? I don't believe them and I certainly don't believe you and your hunky husband. By the way, just how did—?" She looked me up and down. "How *did* the two of you meet?"

*Grrrr.* This blonde could say more with her eyes than with her barbed wire tongue.

"He doesn't have a brother, does he?" she smiled.

I shook my head. "'Fraid not."

The room was curiously silent. I guess the rest of the staff and clients were expecting me to blow my lid. But I smiled instead. "Miz Purewhite, I don't expect you to believe me. For goodness sake, I wouldn't believe what I'd seen if I hadn't seen it myself with my own two eyes." I took a breath. "If there is a Bigfoot out in those woods though, I guarantee you someone else is gonna see it too. Maybe even you."

Tiffi shrugged as Sue Jan began blowing out her hair. But I could tell she was thinking about what I'd said because of the little crease in between her brows. Time for a Botox refresher.

I decided to go another route. I went behind the curtain into the break room and found what I hoped I'd find. Charla always brought in homemade cookies on Friday. I was about to carry the plate with me out the door when a better idea occurred to me. I pulled Charla aside. "Charla honey, would you mind taking these cookies out to that poor camera crew waiting on Tiffi the Terrible to be finished?"

"Okay Miz Lovita." She took the plate from me. But before she took another step I touched her shoulder. "And would you mind talking to the people a bit. You know, ask them where the interview is going to take place and when."

Her brow arched. "Does this mean I'm detecting for you and Miz Sue Jan?"

I snapped my fingers. "Sure it does. In fact, I deputize you a junior detective in our new forensic female detective agency."

"You have a detecting agency now?"

"Well, no, not exactly. Not yet. But Sue Jan and I would like to eventually. We never thought a town this size could support a full-time detective agency, but now that we both have kids, or will soon," I patted my tummy, "doing detective work would be part-time, and that's fine with me."

Charla's nose scrunched up. "What about the Crown of Glory? My job?" The plate of cookies did an elevator fall of at least twelve inches.

"Hey, don't drop 'em. The Crown of Glory's going to go on as long as I walk this earth. I made a promise to my mama Bessie Mae Horton that I would keep Lovita's Cut 'n Strut, *I mean,* the Crown of Glory Salon and Boutique, going and I aim to keep my word to her."

"Whew!" Charla breathed a sigh of relief. "You had me scared there for a minute Miz Lovita. Working here means everything to me."

I patted her shoulder. "That means a lot to me and Sue Jan. Now you go and bring them cookies to that camera crew."

I peeked out the curtain as she left the break room and caught sight of the Tiffi renovation in progress. The Tiff-vation! With Sue Jan on one side of the woman and Jolene on the other, combing and a-teasing a rat's nest foundation, the nasty newscaster's hair was undergoing a major lift. I kept an eye on what was going on, but paced back and forth waiting for Charla, who returned a few minutes later with an empty plate under her arm and a big smile on her face. She scampered into the break room.

"So, what's the word?" I asked.

Charla smiled and chomped on a fresh wad of bubblegum. I could tell it was fresh because of the sweet pink smell of it. She held out her phone and showed me a selfie of her standing next to the guy in front of the salon.

"I found out what you needed to know *and* that cute cameraman asked me out on a date. He had some bubblegum in his shirt pocket and I noticed it and told him that kind was my favorite, so he told me that kind was his favorite too and he offered me some."

"Sounds like a match made in heaven if you ask me. A date with that cutie pie? Woo Hoo!" I winked. "I hope things 'develop' for you and him. Now tell me what the crew said."

She blew a big pink bubble first. "Curt, that's the cute cameraman's name, told me that the interview is at six-thirty in the woods near the old graveyard."

Sue Jan's voice broke in. "The old graveyard? What? Why there? The place is all broken down and creepy as H-E-DOUBLE TOOTHPICKS."

I spun around. "What are you doing in here, Suey?" I asked. "Why aren't you—" I waved my arm, "'teasing' like that salon motto you thought up? 'We tease to please'" I mocked.

She stuck her tongue out. "I come to get Charla. Tiffi's getting antsy and needs her makeup touched up fast. Besides, Jolene's almost done with her. All we have to do is shellac her head and she's outta here. And none too soon for me, either. She and Cornelia could be related. Seriously, the woman's mean as a striped snake." She looked from side-to-side. "And if I hadn't-a washed her hair, there's no way I'd have been able to run a comb through it. Maybe a yard rake, but not a comb."

Charla hurried out and Sue Jan took a step to follow her. "Oh Suey . . ." I placed my hands on my hips.

"Uh, what is it Lovita? I should get back out to my customer."

"No hurry. She's in good hands. Besides that, she ain't a paying customer." I wagged my index finger in her face. "What was that little stunt you tried to pull with Sniffi Purewhite?

Sending me off to the stockroom so you could hijack my story and bask in the limelight of your fifteen minutes of fame?"

Sue Jan laughed at the Sniffi reference. But then she clasped and unclasped her hands like she was thinking up a way to answer me. "I hear, yes I hear what you're saying Lovita, but I was really trying to take one for the team and protect you."

"Nice try," I made a face at her.

"Oh, okay Ita. I wished it was me that saw that big old hairy monster so I could be on the news, so the next best thing was being your spokesperson. After all, I am the mayor's wife."

"Will you stop playing that mayor's wife card? Everyone's getting tired of that. What made you think that hearing the story once-removed would be a good idea?"

"Are people tired of it?" She smoothed her hair. "Personally I never get tired of saying it. Maybe people are jealous, that's all."

I pointed my index finger at her chest. "Trust me when I say this. Nobody's jealous that you're the mayor's wife." I took a step back so I'd have room to put my foot in my mouth in case I said too much. "Besides, after all this Bigfoot 'n Sasquatch stuff, I doubt your husband will be re-elected."

Her mouth opened wide. "I can't believe you said that. You take that back, Lovita. That was wrong. So wrong."

Charla poked her head in between the curtains. "Hurry up, Tiffi's leaving."

That news was like dumping a bucket of water on a campfire. Sue Jan and I practically climbed over one another to get out of the break room, only to witness the back of Tiffi Purewhite's head. Her hair was indeed, perfectly teased into a nice high bump. Leave it to Jolene to give it that lift and volume. I wondered about her makeup. But Charla was real good with makeup. What was I worried about?

"Good job, Jolene."

Jolene had a cellphone pressed against one ear but she

nodded a thanks.

"And Charla, how'd her makeup look?"

"She looked better than when she came in. It ain't my best work though."

I nodded to Sue Jan. "I guess we'll find out what she looks like when we spy on the interview in the graveyard."

"Hmmmph."

Suddenly tired, I sank into a stool behind the checkout counter. "By the way, I'm sorry for saying what I said. That was mean and I can't blame it on me being pregnant either."

Sue Jan sighed. "Apology accepted." She paused. "As the mayor's wife, I have to overlook a lot of sad and unfortunate comments like that." She glanced over and winked. "What time do we leave?"

# CHAPTER ELEVEN

### Expiration Date

Sue Jan and I changed into dark clothes and brought along ski masks before heading out to the old cemetery. Reminded me of the time the two of us, along with Aunt Lila, broke into the Grape Creek Cemetery in Paris, Texas to dig up Sue Jan's cousin Pouncey. And all because Sue Jan accidentally dropped her engagement ring in his casket at the funeral home.

Anywho, we were pros at this kind of stuff now. I brought along a couple of folding chairs. Sue Jan brought bug spray and a few snacks, and we even remembered to silence our cellphones. The only thing that could go wrong would be if my water broke. Almost. There was one other thing though, and Sue Jan voiced what I was thinking.

"Lovita, what if that Bigfoot shows up tonight? What do we do? How are you gonna run with a baby under construction?"

"I did pretty good at the circus, though I probably shouldn't have run. It was pure instinct."

She held up a slingshot. "This is the only weapon we've got. You and I weren't bad at using 'em when we were kids."

I smiled. "I can't believe you brought along that old

slingshot. It's been a long time."

"Naah, it's like riding a bike." Sue Jan reassured. "Besides, if we have to make Bigfoot relocate to another part of the woods, I think either you or I will figure out how to use this in a jiffy."

The broke-down, nearly-forgotten cemetery was located near a clearing in the woods due north of Wachita. The clearing was right next to the graveyard and offered a great view of the wobbly headstones and crosses and surrounded on two sides by trees. Our guess was that this would be the place the camera folk would want to be. The angles were perfect.

Sue Jan had set up baby monitors around the perimeter so we could hear what was going on. And sure enough I soon heard the sound of brush moving and footsteps crunching and held a finger to my lips. "Shhhh." Time to go zero dark. I pulled my ski mask down over my face and Sue Jan did the same. We broke out our binoculars and heard every sound thanks to our ear buds..

The first folks to step into the clearing were the news crew. The camera people started fiddling with their equipment and sound booms and such. There were even more of them than before. My guess is that some of these people were the advance team for the Bigfoot TV show. They set up lights and put out camp chairs and started a campfire.

Next, the stars of the show, all three of them with ZZ-Top beards, showed up decked in a variety of styles. One looked like a hillbilly. The other wore a sleeveless lumberjack shirt and bib overalls, and the third one wore Camo from head to steel-booted toe. And they all wore hats. They sat in the camp chairs and commenced to reading what I guessed was their script.

Sue Jan muffled through the knit mask. "Look at those papers in their hands. And I thought this show was real."

To tell the truth, I was a little disappointed too. In the back of my mind, I held out hope that there was a flicker of a possibility that they really did chase down creatures like Bigfoot in the woods in the middle of the night, armed to the teeth. But then again, I've always held out hope that the Loch Ness Monster is real too. Call me a dreamer.

I know what I saw that night at the circus, and it stuck in my brain like a splinter I couldn't quite get the tweezers around. What exactly did I see? Could the whole scene have been faked? I was going to have to look at this with the eye of a forensic female, not a frightened observer, startled and scared by the sight of a—and just like that, an idea came to mind as I replayed the scene, which pinball'd me to yet another idea.

The stars of the show stood up and handed their scripts to the crew. A camera focused in on Pinkie's bearded face. Show time .

A doom-and-gloom-expression on his face, Pinkie began to speak:

"We're here in the tiny town of Wachita, Texas in the middle of nowhere following up on reports of a creature we're gonna call 'The Wild Man of Wachita.'"

Sue Jan whispered. "What's he talking about? Wachita—a tiny town in the middle of nowhere?"

"Shush!" I whispered, index finger across my lips. But I realized how ridiculous the gesture was. We both had ski masks on. Duh.

Pinkie went on. "But before we talk about that, I wanna read this letter I got from a woman named Chardonnay Mahoney from Kissimmee, Florida. She's a big fan of the show and she has a question that me and the boys think a lot of people would like to know the answer to as well. She wants to know what the difference is between a Bigfoot, a Sasquatch and a Yeti. So, hold onto your beach towel, Chardonnay. Here goes: A Sasquatch is what's known as a primate and person mix, or hybrid. Derived from an Indian word 'Sésquac,' which means 'wild man.' Most of the reports come from the Pacific Northwest and parts of British Columbia. In fact, more recorded sightings of these creatures have come from this area than any place else in the world. Those of us who have devoted our lives to searching out and seeking proof that these creatures exist, are fond of calling 'em Squatches. Now aside from Squatches, the name 'Bigfoot' is sort of a nickname for a Sasquatch. The first time it was used was in 1958 when a man by the name of Gerald Crew, a Bluff Creek local in Del Norte County, California, was featured in a local newspaper. He took a cast of some large, mysterious footprints he found near his bulldozer. When people saw those casts, they began calling whoever or whatever made those tracks 'Big Foot.' The editor of that newspaper shortened the name to Bigfoot and it stuck. Yetis can be traced back to Eastern civilizations in the Himalayan Mountain region. While Sasquatch and Bigfoot sightings usually occur in warm or milder climates, the Yeti is an arctic creature that looks more like a bear than an ape and all the sightings are located in cold climates. Some of the early indigenous tribal folks called the Yeti the 'Glacier Being.'"

They camera lights went off, cueing us that they had completed a small segment of the show. And Tiffi arrived as if she'd planned it that way. The stars of the show stood up to greet her, and I'm not sure, but I think there were smiles on their faces. It was hard to tell with all the crazy beards. I had to admit, Tiffi looked pretty good, at least from a distance, after the renovation at the Crown of Glory.

I kept my voice low. "Sue Jan." The ski mask was itchy and definitely hard to speak or listen through.

"What?" She looked around, whites of her eyes visible, and I realized she was a little freaked out.

"Don't worry, I don't see a Bigfoot or nothing like that. It's something else."

"What?" Her muffled voice matched my own.

"Want to have a little fun?"

She raised the mask off her mouth and smiled. "What do you

have in mind?"

I inclined my head to her slingshot. "Let's take this TV interview in a more 'unscripted' direction." I pointed down. "See all them pebbles. I'd pick 'em up if I could, but bending over ain't easy these days."

"No problem, Ita. I got this." Sue Jan crouched down and sprung back up with a nice handful.

"Now let's have some fun."

Tongue hanging out one side of her lips, which were only visible through the mouth opening, Sue Jan aimed the slingshot at a big pine tree behind the stars of the show and fired off the first pebble.

Startled, the stars jumped up off their seats, cameras filming the whole time, though I knew things were gonna look a bit shaky the way the crew was bolting up and down. Before they knew it, Sue Jan had fired off half a dozen pea-size pebbles and people were scattering like roaches in a midnight kitchen.

I tugged her sleeve. "Do you see that? Those Squatch chasers didn't run after the monster, they're running straight towards the vans they came in on."

"Lily-livered, every one of 'em." Sue Jan replied. She gulped. "Ita, it's time for us to leave. Some of them camera crew are heading this way. They're sure braver than their bosses."

"Okay, I knew we'd have to skedaddle fast out of here."

She focused on my midsection. "Did your—did your water break or something?"

"No, I've got three weeks to go. It's something else. I've been puzzling around a few thoughts and need to talk about it. Let's go to the Lone Star Café and hash it out over corned beef hash and eggs. Just kidding about the beef hash."

Sue Jan didn't need to be enticed twice. We backed ourselves out of our vantage point, made our way out of the woods the same way we came in, and all without being spotted. Once we were in the van, we took off our masks and breathed deep.

Sue Jan pulled out her keys. "Feels so good to take a ski mask off. I don't know how crooks do it."

"Or skiers for that matter," I added.

Sue Jan started up the van and took off down the road. "Spit it out, Ita. What do you want to talk about?"

I licked my lips. "I think I know, Suey."

"Know what?" She scrunched her face to the side.

"I think I know who is impersonating a Sasquatch or Bigfoot or whatever you want to call it."

"Who?" She turned off the radio.

"While we were sitting out there, I got to thinking. That Bigfoot fellow showed up when the circus did, but hunters had been reporting sightings before that, at least for a couple of weeks, maybe three. Circuses and Bigfoot hunters have something in common. They both do advance scouting and setting up."

"True. So you think they decided to make up a tale about a Bigfoot so more people would come to town looking for it and while they're there decide to take in the circus?"

"I know it sounds crazy, but why not? The circus is small and struggling. Desperate people do desperate things. What if the Sasquatch is a tall man in a Sasquatch suit?"

"But you said he was big."

"The guy we met the first day, he's big."

"Trick?"

"That's the one. And I remembered something. That first day we saw him, I remembered seeing something on his sleeve."

"What?"

"A tuft of fluff I thought. But thinking back, in my mind's eye I can see it for what it was. The reddish brown fur. The same kind your cousin loaned us to show to an expert. I don't know why it didn't occur to me right then and there. But my mind ain't firing on all cylinders right now."

"That's right! Where's that fur now, Lovita?"

"Hudson was supposed to pass it on to a friend of his in the lab."

Sue Jan's brows came together. "Something bothers me about that though. Trick ain't nine feet tall."

"Maybe I'm wrong. Maybe he just looked taller. If a man was wearing a costume, maybe the hairy feet had lifts built in and the head mask was taller."

"Or he was walking on stilts like the fellow we saw walking on stilts at the circus. But if he was wearing stilts under a monster costume, how could he jump on the hood of that pickup like you said?" She gripped the wheel.

"Maybe, maybe the guy in the costume doesn't always have to wear stilts to look big. Circus people are like stage people. They know how to set things up to look a certain way. It's all a matter of perspective. From my perspective, the creature jumped up on the hood of that pickup, but as I think back on it, I didn't actually see him jump. I assumed he did. The hood could have already been dented in and marked up with footprints."

"Or," Sue Jan added, "He could have been rigged up on a pulley. Like when Peter Pan flies around on stage."

"Exactly." I made my arms into a circle. "In addition, the moon was big and full that night. You can't get better stage lighting than that. And Hudson and I had upset stomachs. Out of our whole group, my husband and I were the only ones to feel sick off the popcorn." My heart started clanging against the inside of my chest. "Oh no Suey, what if the containers of popcorn they gave us had something in it? Oh my Lord, what if they poisoned my baby?" The thought that I had put my baby in danger broke my heart. I buried my face in my hands.

"Lovita, calm down." Sue Jan reached over to grip my shoulder. "I don't think anyone would want to poison Hudson or you or the baby. Someone needed you to see what they wanted you to see. Plus you were over that sicky feeling in a real short time. Don't worry."

But I couldn't help worrying a little bit. Sue Jan soon pulled up in front of the Lone Star Cafe. "C'mon, we're going to go in and eat and tomorrow you're going to call your OB and ask if there's anything unusual about the blood work you had done. I'll bet nothing shows up."

"I hope you're right." I said. "By the way, don't forget it's my turn to pay."

Callie, the owner, showed us to a different booth because our favorite booth was occupied by Cornelia Barlow---of all people—and a strange man. Unfortunately we were too far to eavesdrop on their conversation, but far enough from them to observe them without being noticed, at least not right away. They didn't see us come in. The two were sitting side-by-side with their backs to us.

Sue Jan smiled at our friend. "Callie, we'll have the special *and* dessert."

"No dessert for me, Suey." I patted my stomach. "I'm cutting down on sweets. Also, instead of the sides that go with the special, could you bring me a salad with the dressing on the side?"

Callie stared at me like she couldn't believe her ears. The new me was going to take time to sink in.

Slender and honey-blonde with translucent eyes, Callie worked hard but looked like she didn't. In fact, the woman still looked like she did in high school, which made me wonder if she had found the fountain of youth somewhere.

"Okay, have it your way, I say." Sue Jan, pleased with her rhyme, lit her face up with a smile. "Well, I'm still having the special with the sides and the dessert too."

Callie winked. "You got it, girls."

I wrapped my hand around her wrist before she sprinted off. "Hey, what's your take on those two?"

Callie touched the top of her lip with her tongue. "Well, they've been canoodling about an hour now. A new guy in town."

"Ugh." Sue Jan made a face. "I don't want to lose my appetite."

Callie shrugged. "Maybe love is what the woman needs to change her ways—that, and a younger man. Even though he's a mite strange."

"He'd have to be." I added.

"Give me a few minutes, girls, and I'll be back with your food." Callie trotted off.

Sue Jan and I began texting our husbands so we wouldn't have to during our meal. Never failed. Our husbands would either call or text right in the middle of a forkful of good food. Fortunately for me, Hudson was working late on his special case, a fact I was well aware of when I made plans to spy on the secret cemetery interview. And Monroe was only too happy to spend a night home with the kids. *For real.* He only looked frazzled when he was mayoring. At home with his family, the man was as calm as a cuttlefish.

Callie returned with our food, a few minutes later than usual. "Sorry about the wait, but Lovita, I had to have my chef make up yours special. I remembered that he told me he'd added a bit of MSG to the dish and I knew you couldn't have that."

Sue Jan grabbed Callie and pulled her down close to the table. "That's it, Lovita! I remember Hudson asking them if they had some of that yellow sprinkle powder since there was no butter. You both sprinkled a little on your popcorn. That's why you felt sick. Same symptoms. Sweating, Nausea. Rapid pulse." Sue Jan, by now face-to-face with Callie, released her grip. "Uh, sorry. I got carried away."

Callie stood, brushed off her uniform and smiled. "No

problem. I'm used to you girls." She lifted the empty tray and walked toward the kitchen.

"Uh, that's it. You're right, Suey. It didn't even occur to me that the sprinkle powder had MSG in it. We usually have butter on our popcorn at the movie theater."

Sue Jan grimaced. "But I'm still confused. It makes sense for you to get sick, Ita, but not Hudson."

I stared straight ahead, numb by what she'd said. "You're right. You're absolutely right. No one else knows this yet. But Hudson might be allergic too. He went through testing with an allergist in Washington after he took sick on Chinese takeout."

Suey shook her head. "Wow, it's hard to believe that two people who are both allergic to MSG would find each other and get married."

"We're waiting on the results."

"I hope he's not," Sue Jan said.

"I hardly sprinkled any on mine. Funny, I didn't feel the same way I did with my other MSG experiences. Certainly enough to make me feel a bit sick, but not sickly sick. Or deathly sick, thank God, more of a go-home-and-lay-down-sick. And as for our little one, my OB said that our baby would likely be highly allergic to MSG. If so, we will have to watch every little thing he or she eats."

"Wow, MSG to your little one would be like Kryptonite to Superman." Sue Jan sat back against the booth. "A lot of folks in town know about you being allergic to the stuff, but no one knows about Hudson or the baby. You three are gonna be known as the MSG family."

I halted in mid-laugh, the second I noticed Cornelia and her man slide from the booth and stand to leave, which is unfortunately when the woman noticed the two of us. She offered a limp-wristed wave and a sly cat-ate-the-canary kinda smile.

Then I noticed something more important than her bad

behavior. The man she was with was wearing a uniform. Her weird boyfriend was a postal worker.

I issued a warning to Sue Jan, whose back was to the scene. "Batten down the hatches. Hide the silver. Protect your brain. She's coming over here."

The two strolled over to us arm-in-arm. "Well, well, well, if it isn't my favorite fatties." Cornelia practically purred.

I managed a polite response, but it wasn't easy. "Oh, hi, Miz. Barlow. How are you? Fine, I hope."

"Who wouldn't be feeling fine with a *fine* man like this on my arm?" She cast a smile to her idea of manly arm candy.

While they were making goo-goo eyes at one another, Sue Jan whispered to me. "The strangest thing about that guy is his hair. His body looks two sizes too small in comparison. I've never seen a style like that. His hair is convoluted into a coil like a rip curl. I keep looking for a surfer to ride the wave. Seriously. And why are two of this guy's front teeth sealed in gold with star cutouts?"

I whispered back. "I think the weirdest thing about him is that he's with Cornelia."

The two of them stopped talking and stared straight at us. Cornelia turned to the man. "Clem, do you know how to seduce a fat woman?"

*Clem? In all my life I'd never met anyone named Clem. Yet it seemed to fit...*

He shrugged his big shoulders, which made his bouffant bob at an angle like a shark's fin.

Cornelia waved her hand. "Piece of cake!"

Like Sue Jan and I hadn't heard *that* one before with all the years of bullying we'd endured.

Sue Jan twiddled her fingers. "Wow, Bore-nelia, we're splitting our sides over that one, ain't we Lovita?"

I nodded, wringing my lips to the side to accentuate my

distaste for her mean joke.

Sue Jan held up her phone. "Why, look at the time. It's getting late." She stared straight at the odd couple. "Don't you two have to report back to the mother ship or something?"

# CHAPTER TWELVE

■■■■■■■■■■■■■■■■■■■■■■■■■

## Juggling Clues

The previous night had turned out to be full of surprises. But when Zeke texted Sue Jan and me in the a.m. and asked if he and Zara could meet with us somewhere to talk, I knew we were on a roll. Sue Jan and I talked and decided to call upon our old friend Bo who used to work at the Crown of Glory. Well, technically she worked there before we changed the name from Lovita's Cut 'n Strut to the Crown of Glory Beauty Salon and Boutique. Any who, Bo and her husband Shaozu, own and operate our favorite Chinese restaurant in town, the Wok of Ages. They agreed to let us meet with the inky-dinky duo in the restaurant while they were setting up to open. That's what good friends are for.

Sue Jan was stirring a packet of Stevia into a cup of decaf and staring at the TV screen up on the wall of the restaurant when I arrived. "Your jasmine tea is coming. Bo said she'd be back in a sec."

"Thanks for ordering for me Suey. Did you notice all the traffic on the way here?"

"Hello Miz Clueless. Didn't you turn on the news this morning?"

"No, I— didn't get a chance."

"Well," she giggled, "Tiffi's reporting that there might be a whole herd of them angry Squatches in the woods around Wachita, thanks to our unscripted addition to last night's interview. She showed some real scary footage of the crew scattering as objects were hurled at the group to get them to leave the woods. Tiffi interviewed the TV show fellas after we skedaddled and they were all wide-eyed and trembling. I think Mr. Pinkie Mountebank is goin' to have to change his name to Señor Poopy Pants."

I covered my mouth with my hand as I bellowed laughter. "Oh Suey, you can't make me laugh. It's wrong to make a pregnant woman laugh like that."

"You'd better sit down before I have to come up with a name for you too," Sue Jan slid to make room for me.

Looming over the booth, I took a deep breath to blow out any remnants of giggling, snickering and such. Then I angled my body to begin the slow slide. "By the way, Hudson heard from the doctor in Washington. He's not allergic after all."

"What? Why did he get sick the other night then?"

"That's the best part. That doctor thinks Hudson had something called sympathy sickness."

"You mean on account of he felt sorry for you being pregsies?"

"Yup," I bounced my head up and down. "The doctor told him that some husbands even put on weight in their stomach area like they're with child, and even get weird cravings or pains."

"Well, I'll be!" Sue Jan giggled. "I'll bet you're glad he didn't put on weight in his stomach area. Otherwise with the rest of him being so tall and slim, he'd look like he's smuggling a basketball out of Walmart. I'm happy for you though, and the baby. Less risk with only one parent having the allergy."

"I called my doctor this morning but had to leave a message.

## WEIGHTY MATTERS

She'll likely call me back when I'm right in the middle of doing something important." I laughed.

Sue Jan waved her palm forward. "Never fails. Now c'mon."

Sue Jan took my hand and helped me along the last few inches of the squeeze into the seat. "Girl, after today, no more restaurant booths until you give birth. We'd better wrap up these investigations fast before you pop that little one out." Sue Jan's eyes took on a faraway look. "I can't wait till you and I do mommy things together. We'll make the drive to the big city to take our kids to the zoo and we'll go to NASA and teach 'em about space. And bunches of fun things. Ooh, and I wanna go in that anti-gravity room at NASA and float around. Won't that be fun?"

"Did I hear you say 'anti-gravity room'?" Zeke laughed. "There isn't one." He motioned to Zara, his wife, to slide into the booth seat opposite us before joining her.

"What do you mean by that?" Sue Jan put her cup down. "Of course there is. I wanna fly around like a butterfly and kick my legs off the ceiling like a donkey and know what it's like to feel weightless. There's no better dream for folks who are pound-challenged." Then she leaned forward and held her hand on the side of her mouth like she was telling the couple a secret. "Or for a ginormous pregnant woman." She pointed her index finger towards me.

"I'm serious." Zeke sat down. "There isn't one. The astronauts go up in a jet they call the Vomit Comet which gets 'em in a reduced gravity situation and it's like the anti-gravity room you're talking about, but there isn't one on earth. Not yet anyways."

I elbowed Sue Jan. "I don't know about you, but I feel scienced."

But Suey didn't hear a word I said. "Are you sure?"

Zeke replied. "I sure am. Zara and I visited NASA years ago, and I asked the first guy I saw that worked there where the anti-gravity room was, and he told me there wasn't one. It doesn't exist."

Sue Jan's face fell. "I've lived my whole life thinking there was an anti-gravity room at NASA that the astronauts trained in, doing somersaults and jumping up and down real high and bouncing off the ceiling, and now you're telling me it ain't so. Well that just bursts my bubble. Thanks Zeke."

"I can't help it. The truth is the truth," he apologized.

"Excuse us for being so rude." I reached out to shake their hands. "We didn't even say hello."

Sue Jan shook hands with the two of them as well, but I noticed she kept shaking hands with Zara. I glanced over and noticed my friend had finally grounded her thoughts on something other than the fictional anti-gravity room, and was downright mesmerized by all the tats that were showing on the inky-dinky duo. The husband and wife couple were wearing tanks and shorts and showing a lot more skin than either of us had ever witnessed before, except during the parade into town.

On the parts of his body that were visible to us, Zeke sported part of a Japanese tidal wave on his chest, some Pin-up women on his upper arms, a red-and-white circus tent with an elephant on a unicycle, a flaming hoop, and a man being shot out of a cannon. Zara had a sword tattoo'd under her chin and down her neck, a sugar skull with daisies for eyes, a flying saucer, a mermaid, a lady in a skimpy bustier and ruffled skirt holding a parasol and balancing on a tiger's back, and an elephant head and trunk with beaded swags across its forehead and plumes of yellow and green feathers on its head.

"Uh, sorry." Sue Jan somehow snapped out of it and let go of the woman's hand. "It's just that I—I've never seen nothing like you two before. Your tats sure are beautiful to look at, but don't you wish—?" She cleared her throat. "Don't you wish your tats weren't permanent? I mean, I wouldn't mind having a few of them skin pictures on me, but whenever I got tired of 'em, I'd wanna press some Silly Putty on 'em and pull the images right off and go back to my regular normal self God created me to be. Didn't you ever do that fun stuff with Silly Putty and comic strips?" Sue Jan snickered.

The couple erupted in laughter. Zara wiped her eyes with a napkin as she answered. "We'd be out of a job without these 'skin pictures' as you call them. My husband and I prefer to think of our tattoos as body modification."

Zeke added, "Tattooing is our expression of art and we are the canvas. It's that simple."

Bo showed up with a big smile and my tea. She poured more decaf into Sue Jan's mug. "Before I go back to dressing the tables, do your friends want something to drink, Miz Lovita?"

"Coffee please." Zara ordered.

"Sounds good. I'd like that too." Zeke nodded. "Could we order something to eat? Whatever you're cooking in the kitchen smells great."

"My husband is prepping for lunch and dinner. Sorry, Chinese breakfasts don't draw big crowds. Come back later. You'll love the food. Ask Miz Sue Jan and Miz Lovita." She swiped at a coffee spill on the table with her dishrag and moved on to a nearby booth.

"She's right, we love the Wok of Ages. Best Chinese food in town," I lifted my mug and took a sip and noticed Sue Jan did likewise. She took a swig of her decaf and stared at the couple.

I put my mug down on the table and wrapped my hands around it. "So what do you want to talk about?"

Zara looked at her husband. "We're here because—because we're scared."

Sue Jan cocked her head. "Scared of what?"

Bo arrived with their coffee. She paused a moment, lips

parting to a fleeting smile and left.

Zara's hand shook as she tried to pick up her coffee. "Scared we're gonna be next." Her eyes met Sue Jan's.

Sue Jan asked, "You mean next on the killer's list?"

Voice trembling, Zara's eyes met her husbands. "We found another note inside our trailer."

"Another note? What did it say?"

Zara reached into her purse and pulled out a small note rolled into a scroll. She opened it up and placed the salt and pepper shakers on either end to keep the note open.

The message was easy to read *and* understand. There were only two words hand-printed on the sheet of notebook paper:

You're next

I exhaled with a whistle. Sue Jan play-slapped my arm. "Lovita, when are you gonna learn not to whistle around circus folk? I had to learn the hard way. I still feel funny showing my face around there."

Zeke took his wife's hand. "We're pretty shook up about it. When I spoke to you all the first time, Madame Curio was still alive. Now she's dead and my wife and I have been threatened. Whoever is doing this is dead serious, pun intended. But this isn't funny to us. It's real."

I directed my question at Zeke. "That time you spoke with us—is that right after you received the first threatening note?"

"Yes."

"We're so upset about everything that we've actually started talking about leaving the circus life." Zara placed her other hand over her husband's. "And that's a hard thing for us to come to grips with."

"Because you'd have trouble fitting in with regular folks?" A wide-eyed Sue Jan asked.

"Trouble fitting in?" Zeke laughed. "Not a chance. In case you haven't noticed, there are a lot of people with tattoos in mainstream society these days. Sure, years ago a tattoo'd performer would have difficulty blending in, but not now. Besides, we're both tattoo artists. We could start our own studio, settle down, and maybe even buy a cozy house in a nice neighborhood."

Voice low and soft, Zara added, "We might complain about it, but the circus life is in our blood. Even though we talk about leaving, I don't think we'd ever be happy doing anything else."

Eyes welling, he kissed her hand, his silky black mustache half covering it. "There, there Zara. You never know."

Sue Jan spoke up as she nudged me to start sliding out the booth. "Maybe you two should lay low for a while. Take a leaf of *ab cents*? To get you the killer has to find you first."

He smiled. "I'm assuming you mean 'leave of absence'? If you do, then I have to tell you, we could never bail out on a performance. The show must go on and all that."

"Whatever. You know what I'm saying."

But Zeke had made it clear that he and Zara would not be going into hiding any time soon. Which put them at great risk.

"All we can do to help you is talk to the sheriff about the threat. You need to bring him that note."

"Absolutely not. No way." Zeke's chest heaved.

I put my hands on my cheeks. "'Absolutely yes,' is what you should be saying. I don't understand why you won't seek help. How do you expect to find the circus killer?"

"My husband and I are not going to the law with this. That's why we came to you. We want you girls to find the killer before he finds us."

I sighed. "You sure are making things difficult. How are we supposed to protect the two of you? We're two pregnant women without weapons, unless you count slingshots. Those, we have."

Out of the corner of my eye, I noticed people strolling by the restaurant. One man stuck his head up against the glass and looked in.

Zeke's eyes twinkled at my comment. "Then slingshots will have to do."

I began the slow slide towards the edge of the booth. "For the record, Sue Jan and I think you're making a big mistake. You're putting yourselves out there with no protection, like guinea pigs."

Sue Jan let out a whoop at the mention of those two words. "And believe us, you don't want to know what dangers guinea pigs have to put up with."

My friend and I knew what we were talking about. The last mystery we solved together involved two things that shouldn't be spoken of in the same sentence: barbecue and guinea pigs.

I heard Bo talking to someone through the front door. "We are closed right now. Come back when we open at 11:00. Lunch specials today are . . . "

I had to admit Bo was a natural at marketing. She and Shaozu would make a mint today with all the curiosity-seekers streaming into town.

At the end of the booth, I stopped my slide and rested my arm on the table. "Before we leave, I'm a bit curious."

"Me too!" Sue Jan broke in. She whispered, "Curious why you stopped. I'm feeling a little claustrophobic in this here booth."

"What other tattoos do you have hidden?" I pointed. "I mean, hidden under your clothes."

Sue Jan slapped my hand. "Ita, what kind of question is that to ask? I can't believe my ears."

Zeke and Zara looked at one another. She fumbled with her shirt. "Do you want to see?"

Sue Jan and I both held up our hands.

And Sue Jan squeaked out a response. "Nooooo. Uh, keep 'em on, please! We were curious, that's all."

They two laughed so hard they had to rest their heads on the table till they finished. Zeke wiped away tears from her face. "Ladies, whenever we go out in public, we're wearing our swimsuits. People inevitably want to see our body art. We don't show everyone because after all, that's how we earn our living. But we might show an extra tattoo or two to a few interested people."

"Oh," Sue Jan breathed out, fanning her face with her hands. "In that case, would you mind showing us a few of 'em and telling us what else you have on your skin?"

Zara nodded. "No problem."

The couple eased out from the booth and stood. And while they did that, Sue Jan and I did likewise.

Then, to our surprise they each removed their tank tops. Zara had on a bathing suit top of course, but Zeke was shirtless. They turned around and Sue Jan and I gasped together. And Bo, a stack of tablecloths in her arms, stopped in her tracks, swiveled around and went back into the kitchen.

On Zeke's back was a colorful collection of retro and vintage circus-themed tattoos. A bear balancing on a big red ball, a strongman bending a crowbar, a collection of creepy clowns, a knife thrower and a Swami with a gold turban, jewel and a peacock feather above it like a quail's plume. Zara's back displayed a jester, a crystal ball with the universe inside, a trapeze artist on a fly bar, a magician pulling a rabbit out of a hat, a lady lion-tamer, and an enormous fat lady.

"Wowee!" Sue Jan stood for a closer look. "Those skin pictures are beautiful, especially that guy with the turban. Reminds me of Jiffy Pop popcorn. But it seems like you have more tats than your husband, Zara. Why's that?"

She shrugged. "I started getting tattoos earlier, before we met, which is why not all of mine are circus-themed."

I was about to comment when my cellphone beeped. "Excuse me." I slid out the booth and answered. As I predicted, it was the doctor's office calling. My doctor clicked in as soon as they told her I was on the line.

"Hello Lovita," Dr. Reed shuffled some papers. "How are you doing?"

"I'm fine other than getting sick off circus popcorn the other night like I told you about. I get tired a lot lately too."

"That last part is understandable, Lovita. You're in your last trimester." She laughed. "That's how it is. Maybe you should rest more or consider working part-time before you take your pregnancy leave. Have you thought of that?"

"My husband would love for me to do that, but I don't feel like I can yet. Though I will promise to put my feet up more and take naps. How's that?"

"Lovita, I totally understand. I've worked through all three of my pregnancies. It's not easy, but doable. However, let me add this bit. You're not in your twenties or early thirties. And because this is your first pregnancy, you might want to consider taking it easy."

I sighed. "I promise to think about it."

"Now, about that popcorn . . ."

I somehow managed to speak at the same time the doctor was speaking and ran over her words. "Dr. Reed, if there was MSG in that popcorn I ate, do you think it affected the baby?"

She paused to let me finish. "Well, ah, the way you've explained it, Lovita, the sick feeling you experienced passed rather quickly. Is that correct?"

"Yes, I started feeling better within ten minutes I guess."

"Then Lovita, after reviewing your blood work I believe I can safely say that everything seems in order. Your baby's heartbeat was perfect. Any effects of ingesting MSG would have been negligible."

I held the phone to my chest and sighed. "Oh, thank God."

I heard a faraway voice say "What?"

Phone back at my ear, I apologized. "Sorry, Dr. Reed. I'm just so relieved to hear that."

"That said, I do recommend that you have your child tested later for allergies. There is a possibility that your baby will be sensitive to MSG as well."

"I understand. I hope not and am praying for that not to be the case."

We said our goodbyes and clicked off. "Did you all hear?"

"Yup, didn't I tell you everything was gonna be okay?" Sue Jan turned back to Zeke and Zara. "I wish we could say the same to you two, but without police protection, all bets are off."

# CHAPTER THIRTEEN

### Two Clowns Down

After our breakfast meeting, Sue Jan and I decided the next course of action would be to pay a visit to Gerline and Max. We hadn't talked to the man since his hospital stay. From what Johnny and Madame Curio told us, Max was not well liked or respected. A stark contrast to Trystan's popularity! The only reason Max was even tolerated was due to his romantic relationship with Gerline.

Sue Jan drove, expertly weaving us in and out of traffic. "Marshal and Emma keep asking me about your baby. They can't wait to meet your little one."

"Awh, I feel like it's been forever since I've cuddled with your kiddos."

"Come over later this afternoon. They would love it."

"Okay, I will." I turned my attention to the traffic. "I can't believe all these people are squeezed into town." I gawked out the window at a long row of cars and vans parked along Main Street. Television vans were everywhere. "How are we going to get to Gerline and Max? I'll bet there are reporters swarming them."

# WEIGHTY MATTERS

"We have to take the chance." She shifted in her seat. "That Max bothers me. There's something up with him, even though he's vertically challenged." She snickered.

"You're really stuck on the short thing, aren't you?"

"I guess you're right. And I should be as sensitive about height as I am about weight."

"That's one of the most brilliant things I've ever heard you say, Suey."

"I'm full of smart sayings, Ita." She pointed to her head. "This here's a bank vault of treasures the world has yet to understand."

"Okay, okay." I smiled. "Now you're pushing it."

Wachita being a smallish town, we found ourselves on the circus grounds in no time at all. But every place in the lot was taken. People wearing everything from hiking gear to high heels were parking their cars and trekking off into the woods around where the Bigfoot sightings had occurred.

"Where are we going to park, Suey? Every space is full."

"I have an idea." Sue Jan put the van in reverse and drove around the backside of the circus through a section of a dusty old trail, to the place where Johnny Roo sat under the tree, and parked nearby. And to our surprise, that's right where Johnny Roo happened to be sitting. His eyes were closed but his nose twitched as we approached.

The scent of popcorn wafted through the air and the sounds of carny music and the calliope ebbed and flowed with the wind. In addition to the circus atmosphere, I could tell that a storm was brewing. A parfait of clouds roosted like doves above our heads.

"Ladies," he opened his eyes. "To what do we owe this visit? Are you here to search for a Sasquatch or see the morning show?"

I dusted off the crate I'd sat on before and eased myself down. Sue Jan opted to remain standing. "No thanks to the first,"

I said, "I've already seen one, thank you."

"That's right, you did, didn't you?" He pointed. "In fact, you're the one who's responsible for all the free advertising. We've never been so busy. Gerline had to hire some extra people just to keep up."

"Did she hire an extra trapeze artist to help Dixie?" Sue Jan asked.

He drew out the word and made a pop kind of sound at the end. "Nope."

"The circus is so busy she had to hire extra people, but not for Dixie?"

"Yup." Johnny popped his mouth like a champagne cork the end of that word too.

"If you all are so busy what are you doing here?" Sue Jan squinted.

He closed his eyes for a moment. "It's my back."

I studied his face and noticed what I didn't notice right away. His jaw was tight and there were dark circles under his eyes. Johnny had his back pressed stiff and straight against the tree.

"Sorry about that." Sue Jan sank to the nearby crate. "Have you seen a doctor?"

"There ain't no need. Doctors always say the same thing. I need surgery but I can't afford it even with government help and I can't afford to be away from the circus, not for one day. I got no savings and no one to look after me. No place to stay. This is it."

Sue Jan took his hand in hers. "Sure you do, Johnny. You can stay with me and my family. You get that operation and we'll take care of you until you're all better. And if you want to leave the circus and do something else, my husband can help you find a job."

His eyes narrowed slightly. He groaned as he spoke. "Why would you do that for me? You don't even know me."

"Growing up I didn't have anyone either, except an old mean

aunt who barely noticed me. If it wasn't for Lovita and her family, I wouldn't know what it was like to have people love and care about me. Her family took me in and took care of me and changed my life for the better and Lovita is not only my best friend, she's like a sister to me."

I couldn't move as she spoke, an ache in my throat gave way to a sob and I wrapped my arms around my friend. "Oh Suey, I could never imagine being any closer to a sister than I am to you."

Her eyes mirrored with tears, Sue Jan's voice cracked as she spoke. "I—I should have told you years ago Ita. What's in my heart comes out at the strangest times. I don't know why."

I turned at the rustle of grasses and soft thumps on the hard earth and saw Max approaching, fancy cane in one hand. *Perfect.*

I was struck at how Max's facial expression didn't match his childlike exterior. With a head circumference akin to a child's, I expected a childlike expression to go with it. Instead, the man wore a scowl and I noticed a diamond stud in one ear lobe. Teeny Carlini was a straight-up punk.

He came right up to us and tapped Johnny on the shoe with his cane. "I figured you'd be here. Back to work, slacker."

Johnny rose slowly, grimacing as he did.

"I meant what I said." Sue Jan rose and handed Johnny a Crown of Glory business card.

He nodded, eyes broken with suffering, but there was something else, a tenderness maybe? Was he touched by Sue Jan's offer? My heart kept thumping emotion even as the man forced himself to walk away.

"Max, don't you remember us?" she asked. "We were there when you were hurt."

"Oh, yeah, right. I do." He held his cane up and tipped his top hat. "Uh, thanks."

"Would you mind talking with us for a few minutes?" I

asked.

"Didn't you hear what I—?" He caught on that his tone made him sound like a nitwit. "I'm not sure if you heard what I said to Johnny, but we're up to our eyeballs in people."

"Just a few minutes of your time, that's all." Sue Jan batted her lashes.

And to my surprise, the lash-batting trick worked. I remembered what Gerline had said about Max. He liked big women. And Sue Jan was sure going to use that to her advantage in order to get information out of the man. I decided to keep quiet and let my "sister" do all the talking.

Max dusted off Johnny's crate before sitting. But when he did, I noticed something that made my heart start racing again, only for a different reason.

Both of pinkie fingers were crooked. Just like Dixie's finger.

"First off, I sure hope you're feeling okay. Are you, Maxie? I mean, Max." Voice smooth as butter, Sue Jan poured on the syrup. Which made my stomach growl because pancakes came to mind.

He removed his top hat revealing a smaller bandage along his hairline. "I'm getting better every day. There are still headaches, small ones here and there, but I'm doing well." He smiled at her. "Thanks for asking. You said your name is Sue Jan?"

"Why yes it is."

"That's a beautiful name. Your name is a good match for you."

By this time, I felt completely invisible. Like that fly on the wall everyone talks about. I remained silent. This stuff was way better than any soap opera I'd ever seen.

"So you're a ringmaster and a magician? We caught your performance the other night and were so impressed. How'd you climb up that rope in the air and disappear? I couldn't believe my eyes."

He grinned at her. "If I told you I'd have to kill you."

What he said should not be scary with such a childlike expression on his face.. But I immediately thought of those Chucky movies with the demonic ventriloquist doll. *Gaah!*

I noticed Sue Jan swallow a stone of fear. But somehow she managed to keep her cool and stay on track.

"I forgot. That's one of them magician's trade secrets, eh?"

"That's right," he answered, "Closely-guarded."

"You're a ringmaster too, though? How do you do both? Is there a time coming when you're going to have to choose one or the other? And if so, which one do you want to do more?"

Without hesitation, he answered. "Ringmaster. I've always wanted to be the star of the show."

"Is that what a ringmaster is?"

His voice rose as he spoke, and as it did, sounded like he'd just inhaled helium. "Unquestionably so. The show is a success based on who leads it. Without proper leadership in position, the whole thing falls like a house of cards."

And then Sue Jan went in for the kill.

"Were you born to it?"

He held his cane between both hands, the tip resting on the ground like he was regal or something. Then he inclined his head to her. "You're a very perceptive woman." He sat up straighter and adjusted his collar. "People say I'm a natural born leader. They can see it in me. That's what I've heard people say, anyway."

Sue Jan sighed. "I feel embarrassed to ask this."

He leaned in toward her. "Embarrassed to ask what?"

"Well, I was wondering . . . "

"Go on."

"If I could. Do you think I could? I mean. Could I have your autograph?" She Jan thrust a small notebook and pen towards him. "Ringmaster Carlini! You're like a bona fide celebrity." He smiled from ear to ear. "Sure."

"That was brilliant of you, asking for Teeny Carlini's autograph and all. Now we have an example of his writing to compare to the note that was tacked to Zeke and Zara's door." I took a bite of fresh blueberry muffins Sue Jan had brought into the salon to share.

"Thanks Ita. The idea came to me, that's all. I ran the sample over to the sheriff on my way in this morning."

"But he doesn't have the note. Does Zeke even still have that note? Maybe they threw it away. Hmmm. I guess we're going to have to try and convince them to hand it over."

"Good luck with that," Sue Jan piped up.

I wiped a bit of blueberry muffin off the side of my lip. "There's some sinister circus stuff going on for sure. We need to step things up and get this investigation done before anything else happens." I patted my belly. "Plus, I don't know how much longer I'm going to hold out until this baby comes. I feel like I'm ready, you know?"

"Oh boy, do I know! I'm still in the early stages, but I remember what the last trimester was like." She pointed to the laptop. "Let's git to our research, Ita. We gotta put some pep in our step."

I opened my laptop and logged in.

"Did you find anything yet?" Sue Jan hovered over my back like a helicopter.

"Hold your horses. I'm looking." I clicked and scrolled until I found what I was looking for. "Clinodactyly."

"What? Is that like one of them flying dinosaurs?"

I squinted. "You mean a pterodactyl?"

"That's it."

"Nope, it's a condition certain folks have that they're born with. It's in their genes, their DNA and their fingers can either be slightly crooked or way way crooked. Definitely runs in families. It says here that Clinodactyly is a congenital defect. Some used to think it had something to do with mental retardation or DOWN syndrome. But others think it's a sign for people who have artistic, creative or mystical tendencies."

"Wow," Sue Jan tick-tocked her head to the side. "Is that it?"

"The word for it comes from *klinen* which means 'to bend,' and *dakylos* meaning 'digit,' or curvature of the digit, most commonly the fifth finger or little finger."

"Lovita," she snickered. "Now I feel scienced."

I gave her a smile and a side-glance. "Which means or could mean that Dixie and Max could be related. Maybe brother and sister?"

Sue Jan sank to a stool and tore a hunk of banana off with her teeth. "But I'm stumped. How could she be regular-sized and him be so bite-sized?"

"Suey, parents can have normal size children, or little people children, or kids with crooked fingers or not."

She giggled. "In that case, he's stumped!"

I shook my head. "I thought you were going to let go of those kind of jokes."

She swallowed her bite of banana mid-giggle. "I will, Lovita. I will. Give me time. I'm gonna have to ease into the new Sue Jan."

"Well, you'd better think about launching into the new Sue Jan. A mayor's wife can't afford to make jokes like that. Besides that, it's just plain not right."

She was about to stick her tongue out at me when she realized her tongue was covered in banana. I saw a peek of it and the moment she thought the better of it. And I couldn't help smiling a little.

Sue Jan inclined her head toward the laptop. "There something else you need to look up. See if you can find a picture of Mordecai DeSilva and blow up a section of it to show if he had or has crooked pinkies too."

"Great idea." My fingers began to click across the keys. "Um, here's a picture of him ring-leading, but he's wearing gloves." I kept up the search. "Gaah, all of his professional photos show him wearing gloves as part of the costume."

"Keep searching, Ita. There's got to be a picture of him somewhere without gloves on."

"Hold on." My voice trailed.

"What is is?"

"There's a grainy black-and-white picture of his family." I enlarged it. "Look at this. A wife and *three* kids."

Sue Jan leaned her face close to the screen. "A boy, a girl and a baby. Not sure what sex. And lookie there!"

The girl wore a trapeze artist costume identical to her mother's. The caption underneath read "Mordecai DeSilva, Ringmaster of Moredecai's Circus and Sideshow and his wife Nellia and their daughter Deborah, both funambulists and their sons, Mordecai Junior, and infant son Michael."

Sue Jan landed her index finger on the screen. "That's Dixie!"

"But her name is wrong. The name is Deborah," I argued.

"The names could have been changed, Ita, and not always to protect the innocent. Circus folk are always changing their names. Quick, enlarge her hand."

I click-clicked away at the laptop and managed to do what she asked. As I zoomed in closer, the image, though grainy, revealed that what Sue Jan suggested might be true. Of the one hand that was visible on the girl, I could see that the pinkie finger was crooked.

Excited, Sue Jan moved the mouse to focus on the mother's hand. "Both her fingers are crooked. And—"

"Wait a sec." I clicked on my history and returned to the page about Clinodactyly. "It's a congenital defect. Runs in families."

"Ita, go back to that picture. I was about to tell you something."

I clicked back to it.

"Now zoom to that woman's face."

As we studied the closer-up image, Sue Jan and I both let out a whistle. "If that ain't a young Cornelia Barlow, then I'm a monkey's uncle."

I zoomed in to the other son. There was definitely something, not sure what, but something familiar about his features though I couldn't put my finger on it. And speaking of fingers, I took a closer look at his. Straight. Every one of his fingers was straight and perfect.

I leaned back in my chair. "The oldest son must take after his father. Cornelia, Dixie and Max are definitely up to something. With Moredecai missing and whoever the other son is, they could be preparing for a circus takeover."

"They want to take back what was lost in that poker game!" Sue Jan blurted.

"They infiltrated the circus!" I felt like the air was sucked out the room. "Even though Trystan hired new people when he took over, there were a few people from the original circus who remembered them. They must have either threatened or bribed them to be quiet."

"Or romanced them!" Sue Jan added. "What if Max cozied up to Gerline so he could take over the circus? What if he planned to marry Gerline, take out a life insurance policy, and then get rid of her?"

"Sue Jan! You might be onto something." I snapped my fingers. "Madame Curio was one of the original members of

Moredecai's circus. So they exterminated her."

"Pickles too, I'll bet." Sue Jan bobbed her head.

I flipped the top of the laptop closed and turned to her. "Sue Jan Madson, it's time we paid a visit to a certain Cornelia Barlow."

Sue Jan bobbed her head, still in a state of amazement over what we'd uncovered.

My phone lit up and I glanced at it. "But let's not go until I put my feet up, have a snack, and call the sheriff to let him know what we found out. I'll call my husband too and tell him and maybe Monroe, because you're going to be busy."

Eyes wide, Sue Jan asked. "Why am I going to be busy?"

"Because Sniffi Tiffi's coming in for another free touchup in a few minutes." I held up my phone for her to see. "She just sent a text."

"So after all that, we'll go, right?"

I held my thumbs up. "Right, as long as you feel okay. If you need to put your feet up too, that's fine. We'll go after that." I lifted my palms to the air. "We're just two super mommy sleuths."

My phone lit up again. But this time, there was an incoming call. "Zeke?" I lowered my voice. "O—kay, we'll get back to you. In the meantime, you'll need to call the sheriff. Good. I'm glad you're stepping up. Talk to you again soon."

"What's going on?" Sue Jan held her hands in a tent over her nose and mouth.

"It's JoJo the clown. He's gone missing."

# CHAPTER FOURTEEN

■■■■■■■■■■■■■■■■■■■■■■■■■■

## There Was A Crooked Man

The door opened a crack, one eye visible beyond the security chain.

"Whatduya want?" A husky voice barked.

"Cornelia, it's Lovita and Sue Jan. We, well, we wondered if you wouldn't mind talking about something with us."

The chain rattled and fell and the door opened. Cornelia, in a faded floral duster, eyed us, a look of suspicion on her cold-creamed face. "Talk about what? Shoddy business practices, or maybe, your ineptitude and incompetence as hairdressers? Or how about your utter failure at self-control when it comes to eating?"

Sue Jan and I dared not look at one another. But to our surprise, Cornelia motioned for us to come in, and then slammed the heavy door behind us. We followed her and as we did, Sue Jan elbowed me. And at once I understood why. A collection of tattered circus posters tacked on the walls of her flat seemed to confirm our suspicions. Cornelia was somehow connected to the big top biz.

The woman grabbed a roll of toilet paper from the kitchen

counter, unfurled a sizeable wad and began swiping the cold cream off her face. "You caught me doing my weekly beauty treatments. A woman's got to take care of her appearance you know, especially when there's a handsome man in her life." Her eyes traveled up and down, as if to emphasize what she thought of *our* appearance.

She removed most of the greasy white stuff off of her face, except for an oily sheen left behind, pooling in her enlarged pores. Cornelia balled up the greasy wad of toilet tissue and threw it against a dartboard on the wall. As she did, she threw up her arms and hooted. "Bulls eye!"

Even though I found myself distracted by the fact that the woman had managed to wipe away one of her painted-on eyebrows, I somehow retrieved my voice. "Miz Barlow, please allow me to get right to why we came here today."

She sat down on a nearby easy chair and pointed to the sofa across from it. "Take the load off your feet, willya?"

At first glance, the sofa seemed to have a white feather boa stretched across the top of the backrest, but as Sue Jan and I sat, I noticed to my horror, that what I took to be feathers was actually cat hair that had accumulated over time, a good long time.

Sue Jan literally swallowed down her revulsion. Her face said it all. "I guess you have a cat. I—I like cats. I have four, you know. Is your cat around?"

She shook her head in response. "I ain't seen Jiggs in a week. But he wanders off sometimes. He's an old tomcat." Cornelia turned her attention to her feet and commenced using one of those contraptions that we in the beauty biz are quite familiar with—a handy dandy gizmo that looks like a parmesan cheese grater, only it grates the dead skin off the heels, collecting the evidence in a clear, removable compartment.

"Umm, Miz Cornelia," I continued, sitting forward on the edge of the couch, "How did you come by all those vintage circus posters? They're so colorful."

She paused her back and forth sawing motion. "I'm a collector and a bargain hunter. I buy all sorts of things if I can get 'em at the right price. I found them posters for next to nothing at a garage sale. They'd be worth a good chunk of change if they were in mint condition, but even so, I bet I could sell 'em for a tidy sum."

"You have a good eye, Miz Cornelia." Sue Jan nodded. "Real good."

Satisfied with the texture of her feet, Cornelia slathered cream on her soles and slid her tootsies into cotton slippers. "Enough with the small talk, ladies. Let's get to the point of why you two large lasses came here today. You came here to accuse me of taking a pot shot at the leprechaun, right?"

"Now that you mention it," Sue Jan stood up, "Yes, you are a person of interest since it turns out you're Mordecai's wife!"

She shrugged. "What of it?"

"What of it?" I questioned. "Your circus, your livelihood was taken from you. Not technically, of course. He lost the circus in a poker game. And he must have had quite a gambling addiction to risk everything to a game of chance."

Cornelia's hand came down so hard on the chair arm I thought I heard some bones break.

"Game of chance?" She threw her head back. "Hah! That'll be the day." She narrowed her eyes my way. "Mordecai was a full-blooded Gypsy who grew up in the circus life. Games of chance weren't games of chance for him. Games of every kind were always rigged in his favor. He had an angle at all times. So when he lost . . ." She nodded. "That's when we knew."

"Knew what?"

"That Trystan had an angle of his own."

"He cheated a cheater." Sue Jan smacked her lips together.

"An amateur with beginner's luck," she barked back. "It's a

shameful thing that he lost to the man. But my husband was overconfident. Fell for the guise. Which made my husband an easy mark."

"And you want the circus back." Sue Jan leaned back and accidentally ran her arm along the boa of cat hair, which clung to her arm because she'd slathered lotion on her arms and legs as usual. "So you." She jerked her arm up and down to try and shake off the hair that unfortunately hung on like flypaper. "You and your kids infiltrated the circus as performers and you knocked off the old performers because they were threats to your plan."

Cornelia scowled at Sue Jan. "That's an interesting story. Maybe you should write a big fat book and get it out of your system."

"But you did have a grudge against Trystan and you do have a grudge against his daughter Gerline, who owns the circus you used to own."

Her facial muscles relaxed as she leaned back in her overstuffed chair. "So what? I don't deny that I was Mordecai's wife. The rest is circumstantial evidence."

"Was?" I asked.

"We divorced years ago, and I took the kids."

"And Mordecai disappeared soon after that?"

She guffawed. "Not exactly. He moved around a lot with the circus, probably so I couldn't track him down fast enough to collect all the child support back payments. I heard about him losing the circus in a card game though."

"But then Trystan wound up dead last year. Do you think Mordecai is responsible for Trystan's death?"

"Who knows? I don't even know if he's still around. I haven't seen hide, nor hair of him in all these years."

Sue Jan folded her arms. "Or maybe we're staring right at the murderer. You could have killed Trystan, Pickles, Madame Curio and tried to kill—" A confused look inched its way over her face.

"Wait, you wouldn't try to harm your own daughter. Dixie is your daughter, right?"

"Duh, Dixie's my daughter and Max is my son. And you're right Miss Brainiac, I would never hurt my kids. That's why I'm trying to protect them. Whoever-it-is almost got both of them. Took a potshot at Max in the car. And Dixie. Well, the killer tried twice with her and I'm done with all the worry. And if I find out who did it before the police, I'll be done with whoever it is."

"What about your other son?" I asked. "We saw a family picture with three children."

Cornelia's mouth fell open and she looked away fast. "He's from Mordecai's first marriage. He chose to stay with his father."

"So you haven't heard from Mordecai, Jr. in how many years?"

"Since he was—was ten."

Sue Jan and I exchanged glances, and I asked. "You don't even know if your stepson is still around." I coughed. "Or alive, that is."

She didn't answer. Just stared at the fabric design on the chair arm.

"Cornelia, did you kill anyone or try to?" I asked.

"Did I what?" She raised her one eyebrow.

"Murder or try to murder Trystan, or Pickles, or Madame Curio, or Johnny Roo, or threaten Zeke and Zara? And are you responsible for JoJo's disappearance?"

"No, no, no, no, no and no." She shrugged her shoulders and strode towards the aquarium near the sliding glass door and began to casually sprinkle the contents of the foot skin grater into the tank. The goldfish seemed to ricochet out of the way.

But that scene, unfortunately, was the last thing I saw. From that moment, the room began to spin. I woke up a few minutes later when a young EMS guy held some smelling salts under my nose. I opened one eye at first and saw Cornelia still standing by the fish tank. The sight of her feeding the fish flooded my mind again and the bile rose in my throat. Panicked, I bolted up on my elbows and managed to tamp down the sickly-sick feeling.

"You okay, Ita? You look like you're about to spew some stew." Sue Jan's voice had a frazzled, breathless tone to it.

"Let's not sit up just yet." The EMS guy gave Sue Jan an annoyed glance, took hold of my shoulders and lowered me back down to the shag carpet.

"I—I think I'm okay. It happened so fast." I looked at the EMS guy. "I fainted?"

He nodded. "We're going to take you to the hospital to be sure you and your baby are all right."

"Maybe some fresh air would help." I looked toward the door. I wanted to tear out of Cornelia Barlow's apartment and write the word "Gross" on *her* door on my way out. Maybe even scrape my shoes on her doormat. Any combination of those words or actions would fitly describe how I now felt about the woman.

Sue Jan, hands on her hips, belted out. "Lovita Mae Horton Taylor! No arguments. You're going to let these nice EMS guys load you into the ambulance outside and take you to the hospital to check you over. You can't take crazy chances."

My friend was right. Absolutely right, and I knew it. I threw up my arms. "If you put it that way, okay."

As they loaded me into the ambulance, Sue Jan drew near and whispered. "I don't know how or why, but there's something fishy about Cornelia Barlow."

The last two words I remember going through my head before they closed the door were, "Ya think?"

"Lovita, I came as soon as I could." Hudson hovered over my

head on the hospital bed.

I reached for his hand, the hospital bracelet on my hand brushing his wrist. "They did some tests, that's all. Dr. Reed is going to come in a few minutes and tell us what's what."

Sue Jan touched his shoulder. "She's in real good care. Don't worry."

Monroe sat in a chair on the other side of the bed. Jolene and Charla were in the process of shutting down the salon for the day and would join us soon. But we all knew that word would spread fast among our friends and the church and soon, the hospital waiting room would be inundated with people probably on a birth watch.

*Could they be right? I did pass out.*

Before I could puzzle out the answer, Dr. Reed, chart in her hands, joined us. She looked around. "Lovita, do you want me to speak with you and Hudson privately?"

"No." I settled my head into the pillow. "Sue Jan and Monroe are family."

Hudson gave the doctor a nod as well.

"All right then." She held up the chart. "Based on your numbers and vitals, Lovita I'm recommending bed rest until you deliver."

"Bed rest? Why?" I tried to sit up, but Hudson and the doctor eased me back down to the pillow.

"Yes, tell us why, Dr. Reed."

"Lovita, you're slightly anemic, which is likely why you passed out." She made a face at Hudson. "Although if I'd seen what Lovita described, I might have had a fainting incident as well."

"Is she in danger? And the baby?" Hudson looked like his heart was about to stop.

"Lovita and the baby are fine. Please don't panic." She focused on me. "It's quite common to be a bit anemic during pregnancy. Also, your cardiovascular system is doing double duty taking care of you and your growing baby. Your heart rate elevates, and the amount of blood in your body too. Usually, your body adapts, but sometimes under stress, a pregnant woman can feel lightheaded or dizzy or even faint."

"Why do I have to stay in bed?"

"The fact that you fainted tells me that you might be overdoing things. We can't overlook the fact that you're having your first baby at a more advanced age. It was hard for me to slow down throughout my pregnancies and I had a lot of difficulties because of it. Sure, I took care of myself, but being on the go and on your feet all day takes its toll."

"You're sure?" I felt my forehead crinkle. "I have to stay in bed?"

The doctor tapped her pen against the chart. "Lovita, I'm not going to force you to stay in bed for the next two weeks. I'm only recommending it."

Hudson added, "And I strongly and heartily recommend that you follow the doctor's recommendation."

Sue Jan gripped the foot of my bed. "You should listen to them, Ita. It's time for you to slow down."

I wanted to turn my head, but no matter which way I did, I was going to have to face someone. "Okay, I'll stay in bed. I'll do anything for my baby. But I don't like it though. We're right in the middle of a couple of investigations."

Hudson grinned. "I know you don't like it, honey. But we have to do whatever needs to be done for our child. I suppose you'll have to do some of that 'armchair investigating.'"

I nodded my chin. I knew in my heart the doctor was right, and Hudson, and Sue Jan too. But I had an overwhelming sense of disappointment.

"Dr. Reed, do I have to stay in the hospital? Can't I go home and rest? It's a lot more restful there."

"Of course you can go home. You wouldn't get any rest here. Home is the best place you can be to wait out the remainder of your term."

I breathed out a sigh. "That's a relief. Thank you."

"I'll expect to see you twice a week until you deliver. Your appointments with me are your one and only excuse to leave the house."

"Okee dokee, doc." I grinned. "Can I leave now?"

The doctor raised one brow as she glanced at the chart. "I'm waiting on the results of a few more tests. Nothing I'm worried about, but I'd rather give you the all-clear to go home after they're in. So stay put for now."

When Hudson was finally able to take me home, the exhaustion hit me. Coiled up with big fluffy pillows tucked all around me, and Buttercup tucked in the crook of my arm, I was about to fall asleep when my phone rang. "Suey?"

"You sound tired."

"Well, I was just about to fall asleep."

"Where's Hudson?"

"Loading the dishwasher and cleaning up the kitchen."

"Lovita, I've been thinking . . ."

"Watch it, your brain's not used to that."

She blew a raspberry over the phone. "Very funny. Anyway, I've been thinking about how disappointed I would feel if I was taken out of the investigation, so I came up with an idea so you can be a part of things."

I sat up and adjusted the pillows behind me. "I'm listening."

# CHAPTER FIFTEEN

■■■■■■■■■■■■■■■■■■■■■■■■■

## "Roo" The Day

Sue Jan's idea was nothing less than brilliant. I could listen and communicate my thoughts and ideas, all through our cellphones and flesh-toned ear buds situated in Sue Jan's ears. The way she positioned them was ingenious. With the phone in her pocket, the ear bud extension cable extended through a small hole and ran up her blouse, up the back of her neck and behind her ears. Her floofy 'Do' hid the whole mess. Sure we'd be on our phones the entire time, but with unlimited data plans, why not?

So Sue Jan set off for the circus the next day while I sat propped up in bed, surrounded by a sea of pillows. I'd urged Hudson to go on in to work, but he promised to call or text every hour and check on me during his lunch hour. I couldn't ask for a better husband. Plus, he was totally okay with the remote investigation idea.

"Ita? Can you hear me okay?"

"Yes," I whispered.

Sue Jan whispered back. "I'm walking past the elephants right now. I've never been so close to an elephant before. They have bristly hair on their heads when you see them up close. Did you know that? There, there, cute widdle pachyderm. How's your knee doing? Okay, I hope. Keep your trunk to yourself. Nice elephant. Whew! Thank goodness I'm past them now. Elephants sure do have a signature smell."

"Sue Jan, where are you headed?" I could hear her feet crunching on the ground as she walked.

"To see Zeke and Zara. I'm almost to their trailer."

Suddenly, I heard her exclaim, "Johnny? Johnny Roo?" Her feet crunched as she made her way over to him. "You look terrible. How's your back?"

"Fair today. But I'm on a lot of pain medication. Did you really mean what you said the other day?"

"I sure did, and I even talked to my husband about it to make sure we were on the same page. And we are. The offer stands. Are you thinking about getting your back fixed?"

"I am. You gave me hope that maybe I could work my way out of this hole I'm in. The pain is so bad that I can't do my job right any more. I can't even get a good night's sleep. Having an operation is my only choice."

"Johnny, my husband Monroe and I would be honored to have you in our home to help you recover. You tell us when and your bed will be ready for you."

"Thanks Sue Jan. I—you don't know how much this means to me."

I could hear Johnny Roo's voice sort of breaking up, but I knew it wasn't the phone. He sounded like he was about to cry or something.

"You've been so nice to me that I have to confess. I have to tell you something."

"What is it?" she asked.

"Do you remember asking me how I came to be called Johnny Roo?"

"Yup."

"And I told you they called me that on account of my missing leg makes me hop like a kangaroo."

"Yeah."

"Well, that part is true. But the way I told you I lost it wasn't true."

"Wait," she said, "I thought you lost your leg to a killer whale?"

"I lost my leg in a circus accident. Juggling chainsaws."

"What! Somehow, that sounds even better than the killer whale. Juggling chainsaws, huh?"

"And I never had a fiancé. I had a girlfriend who broke up with me, but we weren't that close to begin with, so it didn't bother me much."

"What possessed you to start juggling chainsaws, Johnny?" she asked.

"My brother and I used to make chainsaw art out of all the logs on our parents' farm. We were pretty good too. I used to play around with the chainsaws in our spare time, and got to juggling them one day. People who came to buy our art liked watching me play around, and my chainsaw-juggling act came to Mordecai's attention. He approached me one day and told me he was interested in hiring me. That's how I started the circus life. Things were going okay for a while until I got overconfident and started taking crazy risks."

Sue Jan laughed. "Juggling chainsaws sounds like enough of a risk to me."

"One day I added another chainsaw to the mix and flipped the 'on' switch."

She drew in a breath. "And?"

"I missed."

"Wow," she said. "That kind of injury is beyond a boo-boo kind of injury. No SpongeBob Band-Aid is gonna fix that."

## WEIGHTY MATTERS

"No, the wound was so bad that doctors had to take my leg. I was still recovering when Risa introduced me to Trystan. Later, when Trystan took over he kept me on at the circus doing whatever needed to be done. And he kept his word. The only reason I stayed on at the circus after his death is to find out who killed him. I knew Pickles couldn't have done it. I played stupid with you and Lovita because I didn't trust you."

She paused, and things were so quiet on the ear bud mic that I could hear her throat gurgle a little. "Who do you think killed him?"

Without hesitation, he answered. "Mordecai. Risa figured he did the deed too. Trystan fired most of the other people when he took over the circus, except for three of us, me, Risa, and Pickles. Risa came to me one night pretty shaken up and told me she thought she'd seen Mordecai lurking around the tent after hours."

"You mean recently?"

"A couple of weeks before she died."

She whistled. "Sorry . . ." Sue Jan bounced back. "So Mordecai is alive and well? Well, not well, I guess. More like nuttier than a port-o-potty at a peanut festival."

"Right."

"Johnny, I gotta go."

"Where are you going?"

"To talk to Zeke and Zara."

"You won't find them in their trailer. They went into town. There's only one performance and it's tonight, an evening performance, so they have most of the day off."

"Okay, thanks for the heads up, Johnny."

Once again, I could hear Sue Jan's feet crunching away from wherever she had been. "Ita, did you hear all that?"

"I sure did."

"Lovita, you need to call the sheriff and tell him Mordecai is alive and dangerous. Who do you think he wants to get rid of next? He's already knocked off Trystan for revenge and Madame Curio and Pickles because they knew too much. Who else would he go after?"

"Gerline!" I shouted into the phone at the exact same moment she did. We had hit yet another King-of-France moment. "Trystan's daughter."

"Call the sheriff. I'm heading over to her trailer to warn her."

"Okay Suey, but be careful. I'll click back as soon as I finish talking to him. I want to listen in on your conversation with her."

"Tell the sheriff that Gerline's in grave danger."

"Okay, I will. Talk to you soon."

"Sheriff Mel?" By now we were on a first name basis. The man listened to everything I said on the phone, but wanted every little detail, so I didn't get back to Sue Jan as fast as I'd hoped. He dispatched his deputy right away to go check things out.

Then Sheriff Mel shared some of the lab results with me. Apparently, Madame Curio's cause-of-death were the cookies she devoured. Go figure. Sue Jan swore up and down the culprit had to be the skinny smelly cigar the woman was fond of smoking. And I was sure the tea was laced with a little something other than honey. So Madame Curio was for sure murdered. But who did it?

*Mordecai.* The guy was looking more murderous by the minute.

When I did click in to Sue Jan, the line was silent, dead as a doornail in fact. My heart raced. And it had nothing to do with being pregnant.

"Sheriff Mel?"

"What is it, Lovita? You sound upset."

"I can't get back in touch with Sue Jan. There's got to be

something wrong because Sue Jan and her phone and I are joined at the ear."

"Now don't you worry yourself, Lovita. I'm headed over there now. I promise to take care of Sue Jan. I'm sure it's nothing. She probably dropped her phone and damaged the thing."

"You think so? You really think so?"

"I'm sure of it. I'll get back with you in two shakes of a lamb's tail. Okay, Lovita? No worries."

But I stayed worried after I hung up and called Monroe and Hudson and filled them in. They sprang into action and were on their way to the circus as well.

Alone in my bedroom, I couldn't think of anything else to do but reach out to the Lord for my friend who had put her own life in danger to try to save someone else's life.

"Jesus, please surround Sue Jan with your angels and keep her and her baby safe." I buried my head in a nearby pillow and cried.

After a big hug, Sue Jan threw herself at the foot of my bed and sighed. "Lovita, I'm so glad to be alive I could kiss the ground, even though you know I wouldn't actually do that because the ground is, well, dirty and all."

Hudson, Monroe, Sheriff Wilkes and Deputy Phelps surrounded my bed where I huddled under my favorite quilts. "Sue Jan, tell us what happened! I can't stand not knowing what went on. I was going crazy when the phone cut off and I couldn't reach you."

"Crazy is what happened when I got to Gerline's trailer. Listen up while I tell you all about it. It started when I opened the door . . ."

"Gerline, drop that thumbprint cookie, with the luscious raspberry jam filling!"

"What?" The cookie, half-moon bite missing from it, poised by her mouth, Gerline's eyes seem to bulge out of her head.

"That's what killed Madame Curio! Well, maybe. The cookies could have been poisoned. Although personally, I'm betting it was the cigar. And Lovita thinks it was the tea. But just in case, I wouldn't touch one of those cookies with a ten-foot tongue."

Gerline dropped the cookie from her hand and spit out what was in her mouth. "Thanks. But who would want to kill me?"

"Mordecai, that's who."

Instead of gasping, Gerline coughed on the remnants of cookie in her mouth until her face turned pink. She took a sip of water and finally spoke. "Where is he? Here?"

"He could be. I can't say for sure until I see him, but somebody's been on a murder spree and it might as well be him." I gathered the cookies into a paper bag. "Gerline, where did you get these cookies? Gaah! Never mind. You call tell me on the way. We're going to see the sheriff."

"What are you doing with my cookies and why do you want me to see the sheriff? No way. We handle things internally at the circus."

"Except when somebody turns up belly up! Are you crazy? If Mordecai is around, he's going to make sure you're *not* around. Get it? He ain't all talk. He's a doer. So do yourself a favor and come with me."

"What about the cookies? You didn't answer my question."

"And you didn't answer mine."

"They were on my table when I walked in." She handed me

an envelope. "This note came with them. I assumed Max left them out for me."

I read it out loud:

**Sweets for the sweetest.**

"Now answer *my* question," she urged.

"Okay," I said, "The sheriff will want to have them tested to find out if they're laced with poison."

Gerline spread her hands on her hips. "You can go ahead and take those cookies to the sheriff, but I'm not coming with you and you can't make me."

I grabbed my temples and bobbed my head from side-to-side. "Gaah! Are all circus people this stubborn? I mean, what is it with you people?"

"It's my choice. Live or die, I'm doing what I want to do." Gerline pouted like a two-year-old.

"Suit yourself, then." I huffed and puffed my displeasure. "But you're taking a dumb bunny kind of risk. This man is dangerous. He killed Madame Curio. He's a clown-killer too. And he's probably the one who killed your father. Don't you care?"

"Care?" She unfolded her arms. "Of course I care! Trystan was my father." She moved her blouse to the side to reveal a pistol-and-holster fashion combo hanging like fruit off her massive hip. "And if he shows his face around here, I know how to protect myself. I'm carded to carry and I know how to use it."

I grabbed the paper bag full of toxic cookies and glanced back at her before heading out the door. "All right-y then . . ."

"You left her there?" I asked Sue Jan.

"What choice did I have, Ita? Plus, she has a weapon to defend herself."

"Ma'am," Sheriff Mel raised his hand to tip his hat, likely forgetting he had already taken it off inside the house. "Don't be too hard on your friend. I checked on Miz Whipsnade and I can assure you that I did have a good long talk with her, but she refused help."

"Stubborn, like I said." Sue Jan waved her arm.

A thought came to me. "Or . . . "

"Or what?" the sheriff asked.

"She's hiding something and doesn't want the law poking around, even at the risk of her own life."

"I'm listening," he said.

"Let's take it back to the beginning. Gerline's father, Trystan Whipsnade won the circus from Mordecai at a card game. According to Cornelia, his ex-wife, Mordecai was the one who cheated at card games and usually won, so they all suspected that Trystan somehow hoodwinked them out of the circus. He cheated a cheater. Funny, no one seems to hold Mordecai responsible for gambling away the family's livelihood."

I took in a breath and poured out my thoughts. "So Mordecai utters a Gypsy curse that Trystan will die one year later before the first full moon, and he does, from a sandbag to the noggin. Pickles is initially a suspect in Trystan's death, but he too is found dead. Since the circus was not returned to the DeSilva family, the curse is still in effect. So one year after Trystan and Pickles died, Madame Curio dies under mysterious circumstances, just as she's about to tell us something. But she manages to say one word before she passes: 'Silver'."

"Wait," Sue Jan said, "Don't forget this part: The circus comes to Wachita and someone takes a potshot at the convertible carrying Gerline and Max, who is hurt, but survives."

"Right!" I pointed at her. "Now back to Mordecai. We believe it's no coincidence that Johnny and Madame Curio and Pickles were the only employees who were allowed to stay on with the circus under Trystan's new management, and now two of them are dead. Later, Sue Jan and I found a towel belonging to Dixie, stamped with the name DeSilva, which is Mordecai's last name. So we wondered if she was trying to give us a clue that Mordecai DeSilva was responsible for murdering Madame Curio and Trystan and Pickles."

Sue Jan added, "Lovita checked on her computer and found a picture of the DeSilva family who owned and operated the circus. We discovered, as she mentioned before, that Cornelia is Mordecai's ex, but we also found out that Dixie is his daughter. And we noticed that Cornelia and Dixie have crooked little fingers, which is passed through the *Dinah*. And the condition is called Pterodactyl."

"That's DNA, dear." Monroe corrected.

"And the condition is called clinodactyly," I added.

"Right, right." Sue Jan cleared her throat. "And then we noticed that Max, aka The Amazing Teeny Carlini also has crooked little fingers, which means he could be the baby in her arms in the family picture."

Like a relay team, Sue Jan set me up for the handoff, so I grabbed the torch and kept on running with our thoughts. "But there's another son in the picture who, it seems, is out of the picture. When the couple divorced, Mordecai, Jr. went with his father and the rest of the family never heard from him or his father again. Zeke and Zara, the tattoo'd couple said they had received a couple of threatening notes saying 'You're next' ,which could mean the circus psycho killer is after them too because maybe they know too much as well."

Sue Jan wagged her head. "And then JoJo the clown upped and disappeared, just like Pickles."

"And let's not forget about the Sasquatch. The sightings occurred a couple of weeks before the circus came to town, which makes us wonder if the whole thing isn't some kind of a gimmick, free advertising for the circus. It certainly brought a slew of people to town and to the circus."

Sheriff Wilkes laughed. "The circus psycho killer?" He shared an amused grin with Monroe. "You girls have already shared a lot of this with us, but now that you've narrated the whole chain of events, I have to admit, you might be on to something. The bullet retrieved from the potshot incident, proves that the shot was fired from a long gun, though no long gun was found at the scene. We had to send off the ballistics test to a crime lab, but that could take weeks or even months since there aren't any fancy facilities near us."

He wagged a finger at me, and Sue Jan. "It's pure detective work that's going to solve this case. And I'm thankful for all the footwork you girls have put into helping to solve this case. It's not solved yet, but we're well on our way."

"Thanks Sheriff Mel," I beamed.

Sue Jan thanked him too, but I could tell by her face that she had a something on her mind. "I have a question for you. Lovita and I have never really felt welcome by any other lawmen except for Clint Greech, who's off traveling the country in an RV with his wife right now. Why are you being so nice to us?"

Sheriff Mel smiled. "Well, there are two reasons. One, my grandpa had a private detective agency and he's the reason I went into law. He was good at what he did and he taught me a lot. So I have a respect for what you do, even though you're amateurs like he was. Everything he learned about detective work, he learned on the job."

"Sue Jan's lips curled. "What's the other reason?"

"Clint Greech came by and had a little chat with us right before he left on his vacation. He thinks real highly of you ladies and he told us that whatever you had to add to any investigation was worth listening to."

"Wow!" Hot tears shot to my eyes. "Did he tell you my father was a Texas Ranger like him? They were best friends."

Sheriff Mel nodded. "He told us everything. Clint's a great guy." He glanced at his watch. "Zeke and Zara are holed up at the station for safety's sake. They showed up just as I was about to check on Gerline. My deputy's there with them. I didn't tell you all about that earlier, but that's where they are. They told everyone they were going into town since there's only one show—tonight. If anything's going to happen, I reckon it's going to happen then, and we need to be prepared."

"Why tonight?" I asked.

"Full moons last three nights."

An icy chill played my spine like an electric guitar. "And tonight is the third night since Hudson and I saw the Sasquatch by the light of the moon."

# CHAPTER SIXTEEN

██████████████████████

## A Long Shot In The Dark

Sheriff Mel took off, leaving me and Hudson and Sue Jan and Monroe. Sue Jan came over, whispered in my ear and kissed my forehead.

I reached over to my nightstand and casually pressed the speed dial hotline to Sue Jan's phone. She and I had a deal about the investigation, one that we kept to ourselves. I didn't want Hudson getting upset that I was still involved in the investigation. My husband was becoming a worrywart. And Sue Jan didn't want to worry Monroe either. He had enough on his mind. My friend would keep me in the loop one way or another. When she told me to call, I immediately figured Sue Jan was going somewhere to investigate as soon as she left. And I couldn't wait to find out where.

Sue Jan patted my head. "Lovita honey, it won't be long now before we solve these pesky mysteries and you give birth. I can't explain it. I have a feeling, that's all."

"I agree." Hudson sat down on the bed next to me. "I have a 'daddy' feeling."

"All I feel is confused." Monroe shook his head. "I'm not

sure what's happening to this town. Those investigators are still hanging around. Tiffi Purewhite is still here and a whole bunch of other TV stations too. They're all converged on the circus grounds and the wooded areas around town."

"Maybe that's a good thing," I said. And I wasn't just trying to comfort the man. "The more people and cameras around, the more eyes and activity. That means the killer is less likely to act."

His face lit up. "You think so Lovita? Do you really think so?"

"I do. Unless of course the killer or the Sasquatch goes redneck crazy."

"Oh . . . " His head tilted down.

"But if so, we'll catch 'em and find out all the answers and then all these people and the circus will leave town and leave us be."

"But the Bigfoot thing. How's that ever going to go away? Legends and superstitions have a way of lingering over a town."

"Sue Jan and I think they the circus killer and the Sasquatch are connected. Don't we, Suey?"

"We sure do, honeybun." She blew Monroe a kiss and I could swear he blushed in response.

"Hey, Sue Jan," I pointed to her purse. "That paper bag next to your purse, isn't that the poison cookie bag? You forgot to give it to the sheriff. If you leave that around, someone might accidentally eat one of them killer cookies."

She brought a hand to her mouth. "Oh no! I've got to give that to the sheriff so he can have them tested."

Monroe stood. "I'll bring the bag to him."

"That's okay honey, I'll do it. You spend some time relaxing with the kids." She ran her hand from his head to his cheek. "Poor Monroe. All this stress is getting to you."

Sue Jan waved goodbye and disappeared out the door.

Monroe left right after her, which left the two of us. "Honey,"

I asked, "This might be a weird question, but I'm going to ask anyway. Do you—do you think that Monroe is happy being the Mayor of Wachita?"

He paused, and then slowly moved his handsome dimpled chin from side to side. "No, I don't. The job stresses him out. And Wachita is a small town. Think what he'd be like in a larger town or city. Completely frazzled."

"Why did he go after the office?"

"Maybe to please Sue Jan. She seems to set quite a store by the title, and she certainly enjoys being called the mayor's wife."

I sighed. "What would he do if he quit?"

"I suppose he'd go back into practice. Monroe was much happier just being an attorney."

"How can I tell Sue Jan that?"

Hudson kissed me. "Lovita, I'm certain she already knows. It's just a question of when she's ready to let go of her infatuation with being the mayor's wife." He slid off the bed. "Now, I'm going to finish painting the trim in our baby's room. There's a small section left. Then I thought I would finish adding all the decorations we bought too. I know you'd love to take care of the decorating stuff, honey, but I'm happy to do it. Why don't you take a nap? I'll bring an early dinner in to you later."

Hudson waved as he closed the bedroom door and I settled back against my pillow feeling completely content. *Could I ask for a better husband?*

But then I heard a funny noise and followed my ears to where was coming from. My ear buds! I'd forgotten that the two of us were pre-connected. And I realized to my horror that Sue Jan had heard every word of what we said. I stuck the buds into my ears and closed my eyes. "Suey, are you there? I—I'm so sorry about . . ."

In between a steady stream of sobs, she answered. "You're right, Lovita. He did it all because of me. Monroe hates being mayor."

"I'm sorry, Sue Jan. I shouldn't have said anything."

"No, I'm glad you did. You've been trying to tell me. People are tired of me playing the mayor's wife card. I know they are. I have eyes and ears. But I loved feeling important, like I was somebody special."

"You are somebody special!" I felt an ache in the back of my throat.

"I never knew my parents or anything about them, but the one thing I did know growing up was that they didn't want me. My aunt didn't want me either. I wasn't special to anyone then, and I'm not special now."

"That's not true, Suey. You're special to me, and Hudson! You're special to Monroe and Marshal and Emma. You're special to Jolene and Charla and everybody in this town. The world would be a sorry place without you in it."

I listened carefully. She kept sobbing, but the sobs weren't coming as close together. "D-do you mean that, Lovita?"

"You know I do. Sue Jan, you are a bodacious big sparkle of a woman who lights up every room you walk into. You're funny and fabulous and my best friend forever."

"T-thank you. It wouldn't mean as much to me if anyone else said it. But I know you're telling the truth. Oh, Ita, Ita, what should I do? Should I tell Monroe to quit? He took an oath of office."

"Suey, yes, you two should talk. Maybe he could finish out his term. Maybe knowing he doesn't have to keep seeking office in the future will help Monroe feel better about things."

"And he would still be a lawyer. Maybe he could get his old job back."

"I'm sure he could. Or—"

"—He could start his own firm here in Wachita."

"Sue Jan, we really do think alike. Why not? Wachita is

growing, contrary to what Tiffi and Pinkie had to say about our town."

"I love having my husband closer to home." She sniffed. "This could all work out for the better."

"Yes it could. Yes, it will." I felt bad about Sue Jan overhearing our conversation, but I sort of felt good about it too. She needed to face what was happening right under her nose. Real friends tell the truth, even if it happens accidentally.

"Ita, I know we've just been through a moment and my mascara's all runny and ruined, but I have to tell you where I am. I'm parked in front of Cornelia's house. In fact, I just turned the engine off."

"Why?"

"When you pointed out that I forgot the bag of poison cookies, I knew I had to bring them to the station, but I knew I had to go to Cornelia's house, so I came here first. If she's involved, the suspects are gonna congregate there, not on the circus grounds because they're swarming with people."

"That makes sense, but you'd be putting yourself in danger. What if the killer is there?"

"I have the slingshot in my purse. Plus, you're on the line with me. I know you'll call for help if I need it."

"I hate not being with you," I said.

"This time, I'm glad you're not. Here I go, Ita."

I heard Sue Jan walking. Her footsteps ended, I assumed at the front door. Then I heard a knock. The door creaked open, but not much.

"You? What do you want? Where's your Tweedle Dumb friend?"

"Hello Cornelia. If you're referring to my friend Lovita, she's close to her delivery date, so she's not here."

"Go away. I—I'm not interested in talking. I'm busy."

A voice that sounded farther away said something I could

barely make it out. "Send her in."

Cornelia whispered. "Run! Go on, get out of here while you can!"

"Open the door and invite her in, NOW."

The door creaked longer this time. "Come on in." Then Cornelia whispered to Sue Jan, "You should have listened to me." Her voice had a genuinely sorrowful tone..

"JoJo?" Sue Jan's voice was kind of shaky. But mine would be shaky too if I walked into a house and saw a clown, especially JoJo the missing clown. "What's the gun for?" she asked.

"Have a seat, princess."

My heart raced. The clown had a gun trained on her? Was JoJo the killer? I immediately sent a text to Sheriff Mel and one to Monroe, and Hudson too even though he was in the same house as me. A few seconds later, Hudson burst into the room almost tripping onto the foot of the bed. I beckoned to him, held a finger to my mouth and gave him an ear bud to listen in. I whispered in his other ear and showed him the sheriff's answer to my text that they were on their way.

Sue Jan let out a nervous giggle. "Okee dokee. No problemo."

I heard the soft crunch of her sinking onto the couch, likely the one with the cat hair boa. Ugh.

"You and your nosey friend ruined everything."

She sneezed. "I don't know what you're talking about." Sue Jan was a natural at playing dumb.

Cornelia explained. "Sue Jan. Meet my stepson, Mordecai, Jr."

"You're Mordecai, Jr.?" I could almost see her eyes popping out her head like a cartoon character. "Mordecai, Jr. is JoJo the killer clown? How did I know that somehow a clown would be responsible? What about your father?"

JoJo laughed the sort of maniacal laugh one would expect

from a crazed clown. I shivered for my friend. Then he suddenly stopped laughing like his voice had just slammed into a brick wall. "Dead."

"Gaah!" Sue Jan yelped like she was startled.

*I whispered into the mic. "Hold on Suey. Police are on their way."*

Cornelia added. "He looks just like his father. The spitting image."

"H-how? How did your father die?" Sue Jan asked.

I imagined JoJo's gigantic red painted-on lips moving. "Mother dear, why don't you tell them how? Before you surprised us, she and I were having a nice little talk. Reconnecting."

He must have noticed the paper sack in Sue Jan's purse. I figured she'd stuffed it in there and it was partially visible.

"What's in the bag, sweetie? Show me."

"A little snack, that's all. Some raspberry thumbprint cookies. They're kind of stale. I—I wouldn't eat them if I were you."

"Hand 'em over."

"I'm serious. The cookies aren't any good." Her voice took on a more urgent tone. "Okay, don't eat them. I'm serious. They're poison. Or they could be poison. Somebody tried to poison Gerline like they poisoned Madame Curio. These are the same kind of cookies. Maybe poison cookies. I stopped Gerline from eating them and saved her life."

Sue Jan couldn't stop saying the word poison. Or maybe she was trying to get the point across.

I heard the crinkle of the bag as she handed it over to him. "You said Gerline was eating them or about to eat them? Well then, that's a green light if I've ever seen a green light."

"Son," Cornelia spoke up, "Maybe you shouldn't eat them. This woman wouldn't lie about that. She could have just let you eat them poison cookies and watched you keel over."

I could hear Sue Jan mumbling under her breath. "Don't eat those cookies. Don't put that cookie in your mouth. No. No. Don't do it. Ugh. Too late."

I heard crunching.

"Umm, umm, these are remarkable."

"I'll bet." Sue Jan's voice weeble-wobbled. "So, ah, how d-did your father d-die?"

*Hold on, Suey! Help is on the way.* I rooted for my friend.

Cornelia answered. "He-he turned to the bottle and I'm guessing it finally killed him."

"And why did he drink?" Mordecai, Jr. asked, a sneer to his voice.

"Because," Cornelia paused like she wasn't sure how to answer her crazy clown stepson, "Because I left him?"

Clearly he blamed her for his father's death, which put Cornelia and Sue Jan in a dangerous spot. But Sue Jan was bold, maybe because she knew the police were on their way.

She asked, "Did you try to kill Max?"

"Me, kill my own little brother?" He laughed. "Get it? *Little* brother. No."

I heard him get up. Then a door creaked. But Sue Jan must have realized she needed to explain things for my sake.

"Why'd you open the bathroom door? Quit clowning around." Sue Jan's nervous laugh punctuated her question.

I heard something hard thump the open door, probably the hard metal gun. "Get a load of this old circus poster. What do you see?" He coughed.

"Um, looks like a pretty woman and a big, long rifle. Seems to me she's a sharpshooter shooting balloons on a target."

"That woman is my stepmother. 'Nellia, the Shapely Sharpshooter.' That's what they called her."

Sue Jan made the connection I was already making in my

mind. She gasped. "Cornelia, you were the shooter that day, weren't you? You backtracked after you crazy-cursed our beauty salon and boutique and then snuck in the back door and upstairs to the attic and tried to shoot your own son. And by the way, it's Ichabod, not Michelob. That's a beer."

The clown's voice broke in. "Woman, are you slow on the uptake? She was trying to shoot the fat chick, Trystan's heir apparent. Why would she shoot her own son?"

"Well, you're pointing a gun at both of us and you're her son."

*Good point, Suey.* I fist-pumped the air above my head.

"Touché." JoJo Mordecai's voice was slick as oil.

Cornelia spoke up. "I wasn't trying to kill anyone, just scare Gerline into breaking up with my son. I sent her some notes signed with my ex-husband's name, warning her to break up with him. I followed the circus from town to town for a while before I decided to settle here in Wachita, along their route, and planned to send her a stronger scare. I'm a sharpshooter, remember? I can shoot a fly off somebody's arm with one eye closed."

"Good point." Sue Jan said. "But you didn't mean for your son to go flying over the hood of the car, did you?"

"No, I didn't. That wasn't supposed to happen. The driver accelerated when he heard the shot. I almost killed my son, and I d-didn't m-mean t-to." Cornelia's voice disintegrated.

"So you two weren't working together?"

I guessed Sue Jan directed the question to Mordecai.

"As I said earlier," he coughed, "My stepmother and I only just had the pleasure of reuniting."

"You're coughing! It's the poison!" Sue Jan cautioned. "I told you not to eat those cookies and now you're coughing just like Madame Curio did right before she kicked the crystal ball."

Mordecai laughed. "For a psychic, I'll bet she didn't see that coming. And I'm touched at your care and concern, but I have asthma which is why I'm coughing."

"But the cookies?"

"Don't you think it's a little strange that Gerline would eat the same kind of cookies that a fellow circus performer died from? I mean it's a small circus. Everyone would be aware that Madame Curio ate some raspberry thumbprint cookies, especially Gerline, whom I'm certain is preoccupied and consumed with thoughts of food 24/7."

"What are you saying, JoJo, I mean, Mordecai?"

"I'm saying, maybe Gerline knows something about Madame Curio's death. Maybe she baked those cookies herself."

"You think she baked the poisoned cookies? Why would she want to get rid of Madame Curio?"

"Why do you think?"

"I—I don't know."

"Competition."

Sue Jan sucked in air. "You think she was jealous because Max found her attractive? Well, I'll admit that Max does like big women. It's more than obvious. And he did take a shine to me when we spoke. Not that I'd ever be interested. I'm a married woman, though it is flattering that the little guy found me attractive. Madame Curio sure was big and beautiful though. But Gerline seems confident enough not be bothered by a little competition. If she's the one responsible for Madame Curio's death, regardless of the reason," she added, "Then Gerline is a murderer too."

"Mother," he asked, "Would you mind getting me a cup of coffee?"

"Sure," Cornelia answered.

*While he waited for her to return, I heard him fiddle with something in his free hand, assuming the gun was still in the other one.*

"What's this?"

Sue Jan's voice registered disgust. "That's your mom's foot grater."

"A what?" he asked.

"Eewh, don't shake it. The thing is full of—"

I heard something drop.

"—Shavings."

"Here's your coffee, son. I brought you some packets of sugar. Whenever I eat out I always score some extra packets."

*I heard her fumble.*

"Oops, dropped one."

"I got it," Sue Jan hollered.

*The mic picked up Sue Jan moving. She must have picked up the packet of sugar from the floor.*

"Here ya go. You dropped your nametag."

Sue Jan was forever using that line. I've watched her hang out near the beverage station in restaurants waiting for somebody to drop a packet of sugar. But for her to use it in a tense situation like this, Suey had to have an ulterior motive. Maybe she was trying to win over the old snagglepuss.

And sure enough, I heard Cornelia laughing in the background. *Bingo!*

Sue Jan cleared her throat. "You know, JoJo, I mean, Mordecai. I don't mean to pry or anything, but besides me being in danger right now, who's next on your killing spree laundry list if you don't mind saying so?"

"You're a real idiot, you know that? Do you not have the capacity to come to a logical conclusion? Who do *you* think is next on my list?"

Cornelia interrupted, "Son, let us go. You can't accomplish anything by killing and threatening. Too many people know what's going on. And besides, this woman is going to have a baby."

Wow, the woman was sticking up for Sue Jan. I guess

Cornelia wasn't all bad. Just maybe eighty percent bad.

"Cut the jibber jabber. Haven't you figured out that I don't care? I'm taking back what belongs to us. And anyone who gets in my way is going to pay the price. The DeSilva family will rise again!"

"Listen to me, son. Your father is the one who caused all this. If he hadn't bet the circus in that card game—"

"Trystan Whipsnade cheated!" His voice resonated in the small room.

"What do you think your father did for a living? Among other things, he was a card shark. And all the carny games he ran in the family business before he acquired the circus, every one of them was rigged: The Milk Carton Game, The Basketball Shoot, Ring Toss, Balloon Dart Throw, The Duck Pond—all rigged. He was a cheater from the start, and in more ways than one. I struggled to make our marriage work for a long time, until I'd had enough. I was raised in the circus and worked hard to become a top sharpshooter. Mordecai was all smoke and mirrors and he knew it. I finally mustered up enough courage to leave him and I never looked back. The only thing I ever regretted was not fighting to have you stay with me and your siblings. Your father twisted your thinking and raised you wrong."

"You're lying! I hope you get a cramp in your lying tongue!"

"I'm telling you the truth. You're just not used to hearing it."

Sue Jan dived in. "Mordecai, did you kill Trystan? And Pickles? Madame Curio? And did you try to kill your sister and Max and threaten Zeke and Zara? And Gerline?"

"Are you done?" His voice practically snarled.

A knock sounded on the door.

"See who it is," he ordered.

I heard footsteps, guessing they belonged to Cornelia.

*"Sue Jan," I whispered, "Maybe it's the police."*

"Max?" Cornelia opened the door, and I heard little footsteps blend with hers.

And suddenly I heard a surprised tone to a familiar kiddish voice. "You?"

"That's right, it's me, Sue Jan Madson, the mayor's, uh, Sue Jan Madson."

"And JoJo, what are you doing here? We reported you missing. The police are looking for you. Where did you go? Is that a real gun? Why are you brandishing a gun?"

"Hello little brother."

A void of silence followed. Finally Max responded. "Brother? I don't understand."

Cornelia explained. "Max, JoJo the clown is your—is your stepbrother Mordecai."

"Mordecai?" Max's voice trembled. "Is that really you? I— I've dreamed of meeting you. I was only a baby when you left. I used to imagine what it would have been like to have a big brother around. I'm trying real hard to guess what you look like behind all that greasepaint."

Sue Jan explained, "He's been masquerading as JoJo the clown so he'd have access to the circus. He killed Trystan."

"What of it?" JoJo answered.

"And Pickles," Sue Jan added.

"He caught me in the act, so I had to."

"Madame Curio."

"Nope, not me."

"Did you threaten Zeke and Zara?' Sue Jan ventured to ask.

"Again, not me."

"And you didn't try to kill Dixie?"

"Told you once. Told you twice. I wouldn't kill a family member."

"Son," Cornelia spoke. "You've killed two people. That's horrible."

*That maniacal laugh again.* "So far."

As if on cue, someone knocked on the front door. "This is Sheriff Mel Wilkes. I'd like to talk to JoJo the clown. We have reason to suspect you are holding people hostage inside."

*No wonder the sheriff took so long to get there. He probably called in help from the Bentley police.*

"Talk to me, JoJo," he pleaded. "And no funny business, please."

A clown horn beeped in response.

"We know you have a gun. All we want to do is talk. How about one beep for yes and two beeps for no?"

The horn beeped once.

I spoke into the mic on my ear buds. *"Sue Jan, what's happening? What is he planning to do? Sue Jan!"*

# CHAPTER SEVENTEEN

### Clowning Around

When police busted through the door, they found Cornelia in tears, holding the clown horn. Mordecai had instructed her to beep the horn pretending to be him while he escaped. He promised to shoot anyone who spoke or moved, so she did as he said until he was gone out the back door.

Sue Jan was okay, though a little shaken up. And Mini Max? Confused. After all, he'd just met his long-lost brother and discovered that he's a psycho clown killer. Then his mother told him about Gerline possibly being responsible for offing the fortune-teller and that Gerline was his crazy clown brother's next target. That'd be a rough day for anyone.

But the worst part for all of us? Knowing that Mordecai, Jr. was on the loose.

"Sue Jan, I'm so glad you're okay."

She sat on the edge of my bed and we hugged. Since Sue Jan had been a hostage and the crazy clown killer was still on the loose, Monroe and Sue Jan were advised by Sheriff Mel to lay low for a while. Monroe dropped Sue Jan off to stay with me for rest of the day while he and the kids went to his sister's house in

Bentley. My house was locked up tight and our alarm system set. A Bentley police officer was stationed outside our home in a squad car too, and a panic button rested on my nightstand if the need arose. Hudson had no choice but to go in to work. The big case he was working on had hit some serious snags. But he made sure I was safe.

Sue Jan inhaled and exhaled a few times. "Oh Ita, I'm glad I lived through that as well. I'm not gonna lie, I was scared. As soon as the police took my statement and let me go, I rushed home to hug my husband and kids. I'd rather see the biggest Bigfoot there is than see that crazy clown again. That guy is four cents short of a nickel." She spun her index finger near her head. "Muy gooey loco."

"Spinning crop circles," I added.

Sue Jan giggled. "His wires shorted out."

My cellphone rang and I answered, still giggling. "Hi honey. Sue Jan's here visiting. What? Oh good." I held the receiver away for a second. "The lab results are in on that fur, Sue Jan." I put my ear back to the phone. "And what did they say?"

Hudson's voice, deep and manly came through clear as a bell even though the phone wasn't on the speakerphone setting. "Lovita, that so-called Sasquatch fur is a clever hoax. A piece of bear fur dyed a reddish hue and embellished with synthetic fur as well."

"Well. Well. Well." I nodded. "You were right to suspect that so-called proof, honey. Thanks for telling me. Don't bother coming home for lunch. Sue Jan's gonna stay for a while. Jolene and Charla are running the shop. We're gonna have to give those girls some big bonuses." I smacked a kiss into the phone. "Bye now."

Sue Jan held up her index finger. "I'll bet my cousin DeWayne's the one behind that hoaxing. I wouldn't put it past him."

I tossed my phone to the bed. "I hope not. That would be breaking the law. I'm not sure which law, but I'll bet he could get in a lot of trouble for that."

"DeWayne was never the sharpest crayon in the box. But if he did it, he'll have to own up." Sue Jan sighed and reclined her body flat at the foot of the bed.

She seemed relaxed and forgiving about our serious mayoral conversation before she was held hostage, so I kept talking. "Sheriff Wilkes told me they were thinking of cancelling the circus performance tonight, but Monroe convinced them that tonight was their best chance of catching Mordecai, Jr. He's bound and determined to go after Gerline during the full moon. I wish I could be there."

"You and me both." Sue Jan sat at the foot of the bed. "This has been the busiest day ever. I can't hardly believe all the things we've been through. Monroe won't let me go anywhere near the circus any more. He says I've been in enough stranger danger lately and he can't take any more scares."

"So how are we going to find out what's happening? I can't stand not knowing. This is the only investigation we've ever had to back off from. I've had to listen in remotely and now we both have—" An idea burst through my mind. "Wait a minute."

"What Lovita? What is it?"

"I have an idea. Do you have Tiffi's cellphone number?"

"Sure I do. She loves free services at the salon."

"Good. Let's give her a call. It's payback time."

A little twisting of her skinny arms, a tip for an exclusive scoop, and a deal to offer freebie salon and styling services for a month, and Tiffi Purewhite was more than willing to cooperate with our plan to be in on whatever was fixing to happen at the

Big Top.

Her crew came into my bedroom and began setting up cameras and monitors. Sue Jan and I would not only be able to see what was going on through the eyes of all their cameras, we'd be able to speak if something needed to be said.

"I spotted the cameraman who had asked Charla out on a date. "Hey, you're Curt right? I saw that cute picture of you and her on her phone. Did you and Charla ever go out?"

His eyes lit up when I mentioned her name. "We didn't go out on an official date yet, but we had coffee and talked at the Lone Star Café last night."

"Well?" Sue Jan nudged.

"We have a lot in common, and enjoyed each other's company. This weekend, we'll go out on a real one."

"Good." I gave him the thumbs up. "Charla's a great girl."

Sue Jan blurted, "She's my cousin's daughter, just so you know. And she's a good girl." Sue Jan added. "Did I mention that I'm the mayor's wife?"

He stared back, a look sudden confusion on his face. "I promise you, I'm a nice guy."

"What's your last name, Curt?" Sue Jan pulled out a pad and pencil from her purse.

"Wright."

I turned to Sue Jan and we both silently mouthed the word. Charla had truly met Mr. Wright! Another King of France moment.

Once the camera crew left, Sue Jan and I made ourselves comfortable. "I'm so glad you came up with the idea to tease Tiffi's hair, Lovita."

"We tease to please," I rocked my head back and laughed.

Sue Jan rested her head on a stack of pillows where Hudson usually laid. From the headboard, we each had a perfect view of the monitors. The cameramen had set up a camera on us too, so we could have two-way real-time conversations with Tiffi. We realized if we could see what was going on at the circus, the crew and maybe a wider audience would have a perfect view of us too. So Sue Jan rifled through my bathroom and brought every cosmetic and hair appliance we'd need to gussy up and fuss over our hair and makeup. She also raided my closet for the most flattering outfits. We had our work cut out for us, and a few short minutes to get it all done.

"Is the camera light on yet, Ita?" Sue Jan hovered over my shoulder. The camera guys had rigged things up so I could control things on my laptop.

"Not yet. We still have thirty seconds to wait."

Hudson entered the bedroom and shut the door behind him, carrying Buttercup under one arm. "I'm glad we got home in time. I was so busy all day I didn't even stop to eat lunch. And the Doggie Daycare place was busy too. I thought I'd never get out of there in time."

I beckoned to him. "Come on in and take a seat in the easy chair by the bed. If you don't want to be on camera, that's the place to be."

He cuddled Buttercup in the crook of his arm.

The red light flashed on a couple of times, warning us that we had five seconds. "Here goes." I shot a glance at my husband and then at Suey.

There were two cameramen at the circus. One had his lens pointed at the ring. The other cameraman, though technically a camerawoman, roamed around filming the various sideshow performers as well as the audience. Sue Jan, Hudson and I had agreed to scan the audience carefully for any signs of Mordecai, Jr., either dressed as JoJo the clown or in regular civilian clothes.

No one expected him to come in dressed as a clown though.

"That's Cornelia!" Sue Jan cried out.

The camera caught Cornelia in one of the Annie Oakley seats. "How'd she score a seat there?" I tried to scoot forward on the bed, but my stomach wouldn't cooperate.

"Here." Hudson handed me some binoculars. "Binoculars? How did you get the idea?"

He shrugged. "I know my wife."

I held the binos to my eyes with a big smile plastered on my face. *Hudson.* "I can see Dixie swinging. The ropes holding her up are fine. These binos are great. I can see everything close up."

"You know, I'm having some doubts about Dixie." Sue Jan, arms folded, stared intently at the screen.

I glanced at her. "Explain."

"She worked closely with JoJo the clown after her partner quit. Dixie had to know or find out that JoJo was her brother Mordecai. Dixie would definitely recognize her brother, even with greasepaint on, and she had to know why he was working for the circus masquerading as a clown. How could she not know?"

"Max didn't seem to know. Do you think he looked surprised when his mama told him who JoJo really was?"

"He did look surprised, Ita. Genuinely for real surprised. Plus, he was a baby when his brother and father left."

I nodded. "If she knew, that makes her part of it all. She could have stopped her brother from killing Trystan and Pickles."

"Maybe she helped, or maybe she didn't." Hudson voiced his opinion from the other side of the bed.

"Was Dixie involved?" I stroked my chin. "What puzzles me is why she almost died not one, but two times? Or is it three now? I'm confused. And who sabotaged her ropes? Who sabotaged the tent stake? Johnny Roo could have been seriously injured or died as well."

Suddenly, the music started playing. The lights went out and I expected the single spotlight to focus on the center ring, revealing Gerline on the stool smack dab in the middle—on her mark. I waited to see, and to hear, the same spiel she'd used on opening night. The audience would be transfixed.

But when the spotlight appeared, my jaw came loose. The Amazing Teeny Carlini sat in her spot. He wore a black silk top hat that was almost as big as he was. And just as he appeared, a large sandbag collapsed with a loud thud to the ground, barely missing him. A cloud of sawdust launched into the air as the bag hit and Teeny Carlini almost lost his balance on the stool.

"Did you just see that?" Hudson jumped up. "The bag came within a hair of hitting him."

Sue Jan screeched. "Why would JoJo try to kill his own brother?"

"Maybe he didn't. Gerline was supposed to be the ringleader. Maybe she cancelled at the last minute. If Gerline had opened the show, that sandbag would have killed her. The only reason Max wasn't killed was the difference in size between him and her. Being that he's so little, he was off the mark, and that saved his life."

The audience erupted. Screams and panic and crying and people running, but one person in particular caught my eye. "Look, it's Mordecai, Jr. He's running toward the elephants. Quick. Somebody tell the elephant handler." Mordecai, wearing a black shirt and pants, seemed to be dressed for 'puppeteering' rather than serial killer. With a get-up like that, the man definitely hoped to fade into the background.

"We see him too!" A voice came over the mic, "And we're relaying that message."

Tiffi Purewhite appeared on screen. "We're here at the final performance of the now infamous Mordecai's Circus and Sideshow, where a string of murders have occurred and one attempted murder occurred tonight. Mordecai DeSilva Junior, oldest son by a different marriage, of the original owner/operator of the circus, Mordecai DeSilva, is wanted as a suspect in the case. He held three people at gunpoint today, his stepmother and stepbrother among them, before escaping . . . "

Her voice faded into the background as the live camera crew followed the running man.

"He didn't point that gun at anyone but me, but I guess it sounds more dramatic for Tiffi to say three people instead of just 'the mayor's wife'" Sue Jan pouted. "But she didn't even mention my name. Whoa, all that camera shaking is making me dizzy."

Riveted to the screen, we watched as the elephant handler made sure his elephants blocked the opening to the performer's entrance. And if he considered backtracking, it was already too late. A crowd of curious people blocked Mordecai's path to freedom. Cornelia broke through the crowd and faced her son. Dixie stayed a few paces behind her mother.

"Drop the gun. It's over." Sheriff Mel ordered.

That's when I noticed that Mordecai had pulled a gun out. Without warning, one of the elephants coiled its trunk around Mordecai's chest and lifted him slightly off the ground. The gun fell from Mordecai's grasp as the elephant truck plonked his feet on the ground. "Aaagh! Let go of me! Stop!" His face contorted into a painful cry directed toward his family. "I would never hurt my brother. Dixie, listen to me. It was a mistake, a big mistake. You have to believe me."

That settled the debate about whether Dixie knew JoJo's real identity.

Cornelia pleaded. "I know you didn't mean to hurt Max. But you've done some terrible things." A river of tears ran down her face. The first time I'd ever seen the woman cry.

Deputy Crandall, a little wary of the elephant, approached

and secured Mordecai, Jr's hands behind his back. The elephant handler prodded the elephant and he loosed his trunk from Mordecai's chest and shoulder.

Hands bound behind his back, Mordecai swept the audience with a soulful glance, as if he were playing Hamlet. "The curse will be fulfilled. Before the full moon wanes, my family will be avenged. For I, Mordecai, the son of Mordecai, was born under a wandering star." With that, he lowered his head.

Sue Jan and I looked at each other. I clicked the monitor off. "That sure was a weird thing to say. Sort of poetic though."

She clasped her hands together. "More like poetic justice. I'm a poet too. Listen up." Sue Jan cleared her throat. "Mordecai might have been born under a wandering star, but now he'll be sitting behind bars."

# CHAPTER EIGHTEEN

■■■■■■■■■■■■■■■■■■■■■■■■■

## Quatchy Chameleon

In the morning we heard that Gerline was missing, and began to fear the worst. After all, Pickles was a gone-gherkin before he was found and things didn't turn out well for him. But the fact that Mordecai, Jr. was now in custody improved her chances of survival. Fearing for her life, she must have convinced Max to fill in as ringmaster in her place. True love. Ugh..

Sue Jan had stayed the night in our guest room. Her sister-in-law dropped off Marshal and Emma in the morning, and we all sat around the kitchen table, enjoying a big breakfast courtesy of Hudson, the 'Wonder Husband.' Mayor Monroe had stayed at the office most of the night fielding questions and doing interviews with the media. Madame Curio's funeral was scheduled for three-o-clock at a new funeral home in town. Our friend Doug from Paris, Texas was doing so well planting folks there that he decided to expand the business by taking on a partner. And the partner apparently had some kind of connection with Wachita. Doug was in town for the opening. The new partner and funeral director would be arriving any day. All in all, the townsfolk were glad and kind of proud to have our very own funeral parlor.

When a town has a Walmart and their own undertaker, that town is no longer a town, but a destination. I guess Cornelia was right about Wachita being a one-hearse town.

"I wonder if Gerline pretended she was sick or something to get Max to fill in for her. Or maybe she flat-out disappeared. With Gerline missing, Max would have had no choice but to go on last night." I lifted a bit of fried egg onto my fork and plunged it into my grits, releasing a waterfall of yellow yolk. "Everyone knew Mordecai was on the loose, including Max. It doesn't take a mathelete to put two and two together. The litmus test for that relationship failed." I took another bite. Ever wary of the words I used in front of the children, I continued. "And Mordecai, Jr. almost succeeded in 'X-ing' out the wrong person."

"Lovita, I don't understand why Mordecai, Jr. would decide he had to carry out the circus curse for his father right out in the open."

"He didn't at first," I stabbed at the egg with my fork. "But then we came along."

Hudson added, "And helped catch a dangerous psychopath."

"So in technical terms, Mordecai is batty in the belfry?" Sue Jan wiped Emma's mouth with a napkin.

"Probably." Hudson nodded. "He's locked up right now, but I believe the sheriff will be sending him off to a psychiatrist to be evaluated."

Sue Jan crunched into her toast. "I ain't no head doctor, but I feel real confident checking off that crazy box." She twirled a finger near her temple. "Mordecai, Jr. says he's not responsible for Madame Curio's passing, and I believe him." She covered the sides of her mouth with both hands, directing her whispered comment toward me. "For a crazy clown psycho killer, he's been pretty upfront about all the people he's done in." She added in her regular voice, "If the man is telling the truth, who do you think did it?"

"I'm glad you asked that, Suey." I swallowed a spoonful of grits and egg. "My theory is that Gerline baked a set of poison cookies as a dry run the first time, maybe with just enough poison to get Risa sick, but the second time she set the poison cookies out for Madame Curio, she made sure the cookies packed a lethal dose. She knew Madame Curio well enough to know she would not only love the cookies, but also eat them. All of them."

"Wouldn't she worry that some unsuspecting client would show up, eat a cookie and die?" she asked.

"Nope, if you remember, there was a closed sign on Madame Curio's door, a sign we ignored of course." I smiled.

"But why would Gerline want Risa dead?" Sue Jan rested her elbows on the table. "What's her motive? What's her B.O.?"

"That's M.O." Hudson smiled. "Stands for the Latin Modus Operandi, and means 'method of operation.'"

Sue Jan stuck her tongue out at him. "Don't try to impress me with your lawyer smarts, Hudson. Besides an M.O., I'll bet the woman has B.O. too."

After the laughter subsided, I decided to ask a question I'd put off long enough. "Sue Jan, I promise to answer your question about motive, but first I have to ask you something that's been simmering on the back burner for a while now. Where are you coming up with all these detective terms?"

"I've been skimming through old detective mystery books." Sue Jan raised her shoulders. "I look at old movies a lot, movies starring old time stars playing gumshoes in 'em and floozy women with fantabulous outfits."

"I knew it." I sat back in my chair. "There had to be a reason for all those new words you've been sporting."

"I'm only trying to better myself. If Charla can change her life for the better, from a trailer to a pig farm, to working in an exclusive, high-end salon and boutique like the Crown of Glory, so can I. Her success story made me decide to be better at detective work, so I started looking up stuff and learning."

"That's great. I—I mean, the fact that you're doing it is wonderful and I'm behind you all the way, my friend. And thanks for answering my question. Maybe we can watch some of those old movies together, sometime."

"Let's do it, Ita. I smell a binge movie night in our future!" Sue Jan laughed.

"Now Suey, to answer your question about the theory of Gerline being so jealous she had to get rid of the competition, I had this nagging thought that there had to be something more to it than just jealousy at work. So I texted a message to the deputy about checking for insurance policies, because of what Dixie told us, and he must have had somebody in Bentley help, because the answer came back fast. Gerline took out insurance policies on her circus performers."

"Madame Curio?" Sue Jan's brow lifted. "You think she killed her for insurance money?" She grabbed my wrist. "Wait! Now I remember Dixie telling us about the paychecks not getting to them on time, which is why her partner quit. Who else did Gerline take a policy on?"

"Johnny Roo and Zeke and Zara, JoJo, Trick and others. Even Max."

"Even the so-called love of her life?" Sue Jan pouted. "That explains the tent stake and the threatening note and the fact that she was comfortable having him take her X-marks-the-spot place in the ring." Sue Jan narrowed her eyes. "So when times were tough financially for the circus, Gerline did a little Eeny, meeny, miny, moe, to decide who to knock off to collect the fundage! That woman's heart is colder than a penguin's bottom. She knows she's shady. That's why she's made herself scarce." Sue Jan poured more orange juice into Marshal's sippy cup.

"Did Monroe say what happened to Cornelia and Dixie and Max?"

Hudson answered. "I talked to him late last night. They are all being held for questioning."

I nodded. "Makes sense. This case is so convoluted. It's hard to figure out who did what or who knew what. From corporate espionage to murder. Gerline has to be somewhere close by though. It's hard for a woman her size to just up and disappear. She'd have to travel by car and Sheriff Max told me the tire that was shot out hasn't been replaced on her convertible because the bullet did more damage than they thought."

Sue Jan brought her index finger to the side of her lip. "Gerline would have to travel by car to get anywhere. The woman can barely walk. Her feet were so swollen the last time I saw her, they looked like a busted can of biscuits in the sandals she was wearing." She paused. "I wonder . . ."

"What?" I asked.

"If Zeke and Zara aren't in their circus trailer 'cause they're being protected and all, and Gerline knew they weren't around, could she be hiding there?"

"You're right. Good thinking, Suey! Call Sheriff Mel and tell him."

Less than an hour had passed after Sue Jan and the kids left, when the phone rang. Hudson was still loading the dishwasher and I was back in bed, feeling like a big, burly sack of potatoes. "Suey?"

"They got her, Ita. I was right about Gerline, she was hiding out in Zeke and Zara's trailer. Tiffi Purewhite got wind of it too, and was on the scene when they caught her. They had to pile her into a golf cart to haul her off to jail. It's a good thing the Wachita jail ain't far enough away for the battery to run out. Personally, I think the Sheriff should have one of those as an extra squad car. It would be a sight better than having a siren on a bicycle or a Segway. Why not a 'squad cart'? I'm gonna suggest that to my husband, when all this stuff calms down. As long as he's the mayor, that is. Hehe. Maybe I should run for mayor next time."

Sue Jan's voice trailed off kind of sad, which made me kind of wince inside. I felt bad about telling my friend what I told her yesterday. But the truth is the truth. Hmmm. Sue Jan as mayor? The concept sent chill bumps down the back of my neck.

I hollered for Hudson and he burst into the room, eyes wide. I made a mental note not to set off any false alarms. The man was totally on the edge waiting for this baby to come. "They caught Gerline. She's at the station." Then I put the speakerphone on. "Did she 'fess up?" I asked Suey.

Our doorbell rang, interrupting the conversation. Hudson bolted off to the front door.

"I don't know any of that yet. She's still being processed and stuff. I hope she does. I hope she opens her mouth and spills everything. I'm ready to hear the answers to all these questions a-swimming around in my head. Aren't you ready, Mama-Ita?"

"Is that my new nickname?"

"You bet it is."

"Basically, this case is close to closing. We have the crazy clown killer caught. And we have the bodacious, big, ice-hearted insurance money killer behind bars too."

"The only thing that's still an unsolved mystery is . . . "

Hudson burst in again. "Honey, Mr. Pinkie Mountebank is here to see you. He's in the living room. I think it would be okay for you to meet him there. Are you up to it?"

"Sue Jan, you heard that, didn't you?"

"Roger that. I asked the nanny to come in today on her day off so I could attend the funeral service, and she got here five minutes ago. I'm on my way to your place." The phone clicked off from her end.

"Hudson, I've never been more up to it! I just need a minute. Why don't you go talk to him and I'll join you soon." I knew as soon as I got up I would need to "twinkle" as I liked to call it. Being a mama-to-be meant being connected to the bathroom, like it or not. And today was no exception. I felt like the baby was sitting on my bladder playing bouncy bouncy ball on it.

Fortunately, I was dressed and had full makeup on. Just because I had to wallow around in bed all day didn't mean I had to stay in wrinkled jammies with messy hair and no makeup. Dressing for the real world was like thumbing my nose at the bed. If I had to stay there all day as a prisoner of the mattress, I decided I wasn't going to look like I was enjoying it.

Hudson introduced me as I walked into the room. "Pinkie, this is my wife, Lovita. And Lovita, this is Mr. Pinkie Mountebank, President and Founder of the Society of Bigfoot Documentation and Truth Seekers."

I extended my hand as he did, and we shook. The baby chose to deliver a series of karate kicks and I recoiled slightly. "P-pleased to meet you, Pinkie. I'm really glad to finally meet you. I've only seen you from a distance or on TV up 'til now. But I'm real curious about why you're here."

The man had a thick hillbilly-type, down-home way of speaking that sort of made a person feel comfortable from the get-go. In spite of my previous thoughts and notions about him, I couldn't help but like the man.

"I'm real happy to meet you too. Ooh-wee!"

He glanced at my belly, which didn't upset me at all. By now I was used to people gawking at it, putting their hands on it and offering up every kind of horrific birth story and parenting advice there is.

"That little'un is trying to kick his way out."

Hudson and I laughed.

"Sure feels like it," I said.

"You're due any day now, ain't ya?"

"Any day," I rested my hands on my protruding belly.

"Have a seat," Hudson offered.

I settled in an easy chair across from Hudson and Pinkie on the sofa. Without his hillbilly hat, the man looked like a normal, everyday country boy. He wore a pair of broke-in looking jeans, and a cotton shirt over a tee.

"I been talking with your husband here about the Bigfoot sighting you all had. That's why I'm here. Hudson tells me the two of you are aware that me and my team are conducting an investigation here in Wachita, We're looking for proof in the puddin' so to speak, proof that Bigfoots exist."

"That night at the circus, opening night, we thought we saw one."

He squinched his eyes a bit. "Thought you saw one? You changed your mind about what you saw?"

"We were sure of what we saw at the time. But now," I glanced at Hudson, "We're not so certain the whole thing isn't a hoax. I remember seeing a fluff of some reddish hair or animal fur on Trick, one of the circus workers when Sue Jan and I visited the circus grounds the day they were setting up. At the time, neither one of us thought much about it, but later, when Sue Jan's cousin DeWayne produced what he called 'Bigfoot proof'—"

"Can I see it?" He leaned forward.

Hudson stood and made his way to his briefcase to retrieve it.

"So that's why you're here."

"Like I said Lovita we're truth-seekers, looking for proof of what we know is true. I seen and heard and experienced a lot of strange stuff in the woods. And after we were attacked the other night I know for a fact there's Bigfoot activity here in your town."

I gulped. "Well, about that night, umm, I have a confession to make. Sue Jan and I were observing the film crew and decided to have a little fun. Bigfoots were not responsible for pitching pebbles at you and your crew. The real culprit was Sue Jan and me, and our slingshot."

He stared straight ahead, like I'd sucker-punched him with my words. "You mean that whole thing was a prank? You pranked us?"

"No, it wasn't like that at all. We were there to observe. We're forensic females."

"You study dead people?" A look of disgust puckered his face.

"No, we're detectives, amateur ones, but we're not too bad at it."

Hudson returned and handed Pinkie the fur. "I had it tested at a reputable lab. It's a fake. Bear fur mixed with synthetic."

Pinkie ran his fingers through it, and then brought it to his nose and sniffed. "I could have told you all that without going to a fancy lab. This fur smells bad, but not squatchy-bad. Believe me when I tell you this, you haven't experienced a bad smell till you've smelled a real Sasquatch." He handed the fur back to Hudson. "What I just heard from you two about this piece of evidence is disappointing. But there have been a whole lot of reports in the area."

Hudson spoke up. "Yes, there have been an inordinate number of reports in the area, but I find that quite odd. Less than a month ago, there weren't any reports. Some of the sightings might be attributed to panic. People seem to want to jump on the bandwagon when reports like this occur, so they attribute supernatural characteristics to completely natural occurrences."

Pinkie tapped on the coffee table. "True, true. But what we do is sift through all that stuff and," he held his index finger up, "after all that, there's always a small percentage that can't be explained. That's why we do what we do. For that one or two percent of things that happen that nobody can explain. We want to take the mystery out of the story and find out what's true."

I marveled at the man's words. "You really are smarter than you come off as on the show."

"Little lady, I'm gonna take that as a compliment." He winked, and one bushy eyebrow descended as he did.

Sue Jan opened the front door. "Oh, sorry," She leaned against the doorjamb, breathing heavy. "I got here as fast as I could."

At first I thought Sue Jan was simply overexcited about meeting a television personality, but when I saw the look on her face, I realized there was more.

# CHAPTER NINETEEN

■■■■■■■■■■■■■■■■■■■■■■■■■

## Six-Feet Blunder

"There's been a Big-Foot sighting!" Sue Jan skidded through the front door, still breathless.

Pinkie jumped off the couch, his face pink with excitement. "Where and by who?"

"I heard it on the car radio. Apparently, the creature was seen in broad daylight stumbling along an old dirt logging road. One of the hunters the reporter talked to said they thought it might be injured or something because of the way it's walking."

Mumbling a hasty goodbye, Pinkie ran out the front door, hat back on his head, cellphone to his ear.

Sue Jan slammed the door behind her and threw her weight against it. "Ita, Hudson, what if Bigfoots are real?"

"Sasquatches?" he asked.

She threw her arms up in the air. "Duh!"

I shook my head. "Monsters on the loose, whether make believe or not, don't worry me. What I'm really thinking about right at this moment is that I want to attend Madame Curio's funeral service. Hudson, I want to go. I have to go out anyway for an end-of-the-day doctor's visit, so can't we stop by and pay our respects?" I batted my lashes like a butterfly hepped up on Mountain Dew.

He pressed his lips together as if he was thinking about it, weighing the ups and downs of things. "All right." He sighed. "I already knew you were going to ask."

"How?"

He sat down next to me and put his arm around my shoulder. "Because I know you, honey. Plus, you're wearing black. I mean, when I saw you come out wearing black from head-to-toe this morning, that sort of clued me in."

"Awh, ain't that sweet!" Sue Jan sighed. "I mean it, seeing the two of you together is like beans and rice and everything nice, with a side order of honey ham with that crispy crust on top." She brought her hands to her temple. "Oh I don't even know what I'm saying anymore. Pregnancy has already hijacked my brain!" She readjusted her purse strap on her shoulder, reached into her purse and pulled out her slingshot. "C'mon, let's go. I'm armed and ready."

We pulled up to the new Graves and Grooves Funeral Home, set in an old storefront I was familiar with. Sue Jan, Hudson and I walked up to the front entrance. Ever vigilant, Sue Jan had her slingshot out, the rubber pulled back, aimed and armed with small pebbles. She spun her body around like she was part of some elite military unit or special SWAT team member. She swiveled and jumped to the north, to the south, to the east, to the west.

"All's clear. Let's proceed inside."

An amused smile on Hudson's face, he responded. "Thanks." He opened the door and we stepped inside. Our undertaker friend, Doug Graves stood in the marble foyer waiting to greet and direct people.

"Doug!" I embraced him. "I'm so glad to see you. When Sue Jan and I heard you were opening a new place right here in Wachita, we could hardly believe it."

Sue Jan hugged him too, which was sort of a big deal. We didn't get along at all with Doug when we first met him. But then, what funeral director wouldn't have been annoyed if someone dug up one of their graves? Sue Jan's engagement ring wasn't going to dig itself out of that grave in Paris, Texas.

"It does look nice in here. You really gussied it up good." Sue Jan swiveled to look around. "You know this used to be a pizza parlor."

His eyes opened up wider and he brought a finger to his lips, the universal funeral staff signal for a guest to shush his or her voice to a lower volume.

But Sue Jan continued. "Do you still use the same oven for creamy-ation? Or did you have to bring in a fancier one?"

He whispered. "Certainly not! And we don't call them ovens. We implement special crematory chambers for that purpose. Miss Curio did not wish to be cremated. She chose to be interred in a traditional manner." He gestured toward two double doors. "May I show you inside?"

Sue Jan whispered in my ear. "Lovita, getting creameated used to be an option I considered for the far far future, but now I'm not so sure. The last thing I want when the time comes for kingdom come, is to wind up on an old pizza paddle being shoved into a hot oven."

"Okay Suey. Hopefully that's not something we'll have to think about for a long, long, long time."

He opened the doors to reveal a large chapel filled with a blend of Wachitians and circus folk. Zeke and Zara waved to us from some chairs in the front. So did the Asian Yo-Yo guy, who went by the name You-You, the Yo-Yo Guy. Clever. Johnny Roo gave us a sort of salute as we settled into some chairs nearby. Noticeably missing? Cornelia Barlow, which I assumed to be her maiden name; Max, better known as The Amazing Teeny Carlini; Dixie; Gerline; and curiously enough, Trick.

Hudson remained seated while Sue Jan and I approached the open casket, though what Madame Curio was to be laid to rest in could hardly be described as just an ordinary casket. Doug approached from behind, rested his hands on our shoulders and began a whispered conversation.

"Ladies, I expect you're wondering about the custom casket Madame Curio is being laid to rest in."

"Um, yeah, it's certainly unusual," I said. The truth is, I couldn't take my eyes off it. Madame Curio lay in repose in a huge crate-like box stained to a lovely honey-wood hue.

"It's totally custom." The slight funeral-director smile on his face probably represented a tiny fraction of how happy he really was. "I'm pretty proud of it. We had to do a lot of finagling to find a casket big enough to house her. One of my staff finally located a container large enough to serve our purpose without having an industrial vibe. It's an old piano case. Can you believe it? Cost a pretty penny too, but the woman apparently saved for her funeral ceremony."

What he said perked my interest. "You said she saved up? When a younger person saves up for their funeral, in your experience does that usually mean they're worried about their health or know something about their time left on this earth?"

He nodded. "Most definitely. But she was morbidly obese. Maybe her doctors told her she wouldn't be around very long if she continued to maintain her weight, and she took what they said seriously."

I nodded. "Makes sense."

Sue Jan wagged her head. "Even though she's blessing the world with her heels now, Madame Curio's still beautiful. You did a good job with her makeup. Risa has such a pretty face, *had* a pretty face. And now she looks like she could just get up and walk away. I can't get over how her cheeks are so pink." She walked closer to the casket, resting one arm on the side, wiping tears with the other. "Lovita, you know how emotional you were the day she—she passed? Well, now I'm feeling that way."

"Ladies," Doug urged, "Please take your seats. The service will be brief. Madame Curio left explicit instructions."

We obeyed, dutifully returning to our seats, but I leaned over and whispered to Sue Jan. "Don't you think it's a bit odd that such a young woman would plan her own funeral to the last detail?"

"Of course I think it's weird," she answered, "Until today, I've never really thought about planning my own funeral. But," she gestured at a big picture of Madame Curio on an easel, "It's not a bad idea. I'd spin over in my grave if someone put up a terrible picture of me like that." Sue Jan pointed.

Sue Jan was right. Whoever 'picked the pic' of Risa AKA Madame Curio for display, chose the worst shot of the woman, probably in her entire life. A glamour shot from the 80s. Cowboy glam. With sparkle star earrings.

"And seeing that," she used her thumb to point, "Makes me wonder about what picture they sent to the newspaper obituary column."

"I don't think she cares about that stuff any more, Sue Jan," I said.

Hudson brought a finger to his lips and shook his head. But Sue Jan and I were on a roll, or maybe in a roll or a tailspin of some sort. We couldn't stop if we wanted to.

"You don't think she cares? Of course she does! What woman wouldn't care about how she looks whether in the here-and-now or the hereafter?" She folded her arms. "I know I would. And I'm all about leaving instructions behind."

I shook my head. "No way. We're gonna have brand new perfect bodies in heaven, and wear white linen and be one big happy family, and sing praises to God for all eternity. I doubt you would care if somebody picked out the absolute worst picture of you to put on display, although I do happen to have that particular picture in my possession."

"What?" Her face blanched. "Not the one of me with all the acne when I was clowning around and lined up corn nuts over my teeth and put on my aunt's old cat-eye glasses?"

"That's the one." I flashed her a Cheshire Cat smile.

My husband tugged at my sleeve.

"Lovita, you're gonna give me that picture! You hear me?"

"Nope." I folded my arms.

"Lovita. You're a kind and nice and loving friend and you want to give me that picture."

I squinted. "Are you trying to use some kind of Jedi mind trick on me? 'Cause if you are, you do know that only works in the movies, right? Real people can't do that sort of thing."

She stuck her tongue out at me. "Well butter my biscuit and call me sassy."

And it was at that point that the two of us realized the whole place was listening in on what we were saying. If the terrible 80s picture hadn't ruined Madame Curio's expectations of the perfect sendoff, our ridiculous conversation sure had.

We both hunched over in our seats mouthing 'sorry' as we did. Hudson eyed me and lined up his head straightforward with Doug, who stood at the podium with a stern look on his face.

"Friends, we meet here today at the brand new Graves and Grooves Funeral Home and Crematory, owned by me, Douglas Graves, and my new business partner, Gwendolyn H. Grooves, to honor and pay tribute to Risa Markham, better known to many of you and to audiences all over the United States as Madame Curio, a celebrated circus fortune-teller."

Sue Jan elbowed me and whispered. "It's just like Doug to sneak in a funeral home advertisement right in the middle of her service."

He continued. "She was the only surviving middle child in a family of three who ironically, grew up to be a medium. She plied her trade at Mordecai's Circus and Slide, *err,* I mean, Sideshow. And she always said how much she enjoyed working with the public. Risa was a trapeze artist for many years with her best friend and fellow trapeze artist, Dixie DeSilva. But Risa experienced a horrific fall while performing one day, sustaining severe knee and back injuries, and had to shift to a sudden and unexpected career change. Risa wasn't a religious woman, but to the people who knew and worked with her, she was well-respected, reliable, kind, generous and loving . . ."

No elbowing was required to get one another's attention. Sue Jan and I stared at each other in amazement. So Risa started out like Dixie. No wonder they remained close friends. Risa must have packed on the pounds after her injury. Made sense.

Before we knew it, the funeral service was over and the grand piano casket closed. We piled out of the funeral home and into our cars. Normally cars follow a fancy black limo bearing the casket to the funeral plot in the cemetery. But Madame Curio's casket was bigger than a refrigerator and slightly smaller than a motorboat, so the funeral director had to improvise. Her piano-case casket was loaded onto one of the small flat trailers Wachita always uses in their parades down Main Street, and pulled by a tow truck. It wasn't fancy or dignified, but sure got the job done. We were all seated near the gravesite at the cemetery in record time.

I felt thankful that the baby wasn't kicking as much. Instead, my stomach felt a bit jumpy and jerky the whole time we were at the funeral home, and even now at the cemetery. The last thing I wanted was a case of food poisoning. But thinking back to everything I'd eaten in the past twenty-four to forty-eight hours, I couldn't put my finger on any suspect food. Hudson had prepared every delicious home-cooked meal for me, from breakfast to dinner. Plus, I didn't feel nauseous.

Hudson squeezed my hand as we watched intently. The casket was placed over the plot and lowered down into the hole. But just as the casket hit dirt, I noticed a brownish blob on the edge of the wooded area surrounding the cemetery grounds. A blob that moved and grew more pronounced as it approached in a wobbly fashion.

"Look!" A man stood pointing and shouting. "It's the Bigfoot, and it's coming this way!"

The response was immediate, with screams, shouts, crying, and running. People jumped up and scattered in a dozen different directions, knocking over chairs and other people in the process. But Sue Jan and Hudson and I stayed where we were and watched the familiar creature approach. I pretended not to be scared but Sue Jan dug her fingernails into my knee, a subtle hint about how flipped out she really was. I brushed her off.

The blob or Bigfoot creature kept moving forward, heading towards us. About nine feet in height, the same guestimate I'd offered that first night of the full moon when Hudson and I saw it. *Check.* Reddish-brownish fur. *Check.* Stumbling and wobbling as it strode forward? *Hmmm.*

Sue Jan stood. "That thing is walking right toward the—the grave."

And before anyone could say 'Sasquatchewan' the bumbling Bigfoot stumbled over a shovel and plunged into the open grave!

The three of us and some other brave souls, including Doug, hustled over to the edge of the gravesite. Doug aimed a penlight plucked from his handkerchief pocket, and what the extra light revealed took my breath away.

There sprawled into two distinct heaps were Trick and Max!

Both drunker than Cooter Brown.

Doug moved his chin back and forth. "I should have known there'd be some kind of drama with you girls involved in this funeral. Never a dull moment."

Sue Jan cupped her hands and shouted into the hole. "Are you two guys pretending to be Bigfoot? Or is one of you Bigfoot and the other one Littlefoot? Teeheehee. I'm real confused. And why you're both so wasted?"

Max had a ridiculous smile on his tiny face. "M-my lady,' he hiccoughed, "Left me." He wobbled and fell over.

Sue Jan cupped her hands over her mouth again and yelled. "What about you? Trick?"

Trick moved his mouth, but the words came out in delayed fashion, sort of like an old dubbed Godzilla movie. "I jus' likes to drink."

My mind was doing somersaults, kind of like my stomach. "Everything makes sense now. Gerline came up with not one, but two ideas to bring life to the failing circus. The first was to take out insurance policies on key circus people and knock them off as needed. The second was to hoax Bigfoot sightings in certain towns along the circus route. When curiosity-seekers would come to town, they'd head for the circus too. After all, the Sideshow boasted about having samples of real Bigfoot hair. I never made it to the Sideshow, but I would be willing to bet the hair on display looks very similar to the sample we got from DeWayne."

"I agree, honey." Hudson's brows creased together. "And seeing these two men explains how the so-called creature could be nine feet tall. Trick is already almost six and a half feet tall. With Max on his shoulders, he became a veritable giant. The furry costume matched the claims of other Bigfoot sightings, and those crazy shoes Trick is wearing would leave the proper footprints in the soft earth."

I glanced down. Doug noticed and pointed his penlight down

to help me see better. "Ah yes, big hairy shoes. Hudson, you have a sharp eye."

My husband continued, "All Trick had to do was let out a strange howl here and there, and the legend of a wandering apelike creature in the area was entrenched."

"Good forensic work, honey." I kissed his cheek.

"Help," Max's mini voice sounded desperate from the dark hole. "Throw me a rope, willya?"

Doug shouted back. "The police are on the way, Mr. Bigfoot. They'll hoist you out."

"Throw me. Throw me a rope, willya?" he begged.

Doug narrowed his eyes at me. "What's he talking about?"

"He's a magician. The man is probably so drunk he thinks that the old rope trick will work to get him out."

Doug cupped his hands and was about to yell back a reply when I let loose an operatic-worthy scream.

"OH NO." I looked down. "My water just broke!"

# CHAPTER TWENTY

## Small Things

"Push, push!" Sue Jan's mouth seemed to move in slow motion, her face contorted.

I looked to my left, past the surgical drapes covering the lower half of my body. Hudson leaned towards me, his mouth slow-moving too. Urging me to push. I tried, or at least I thought so. My body wouldn't respond in a normal way. I moved my face to the side, tears streaming down. "I wish this part was over with!"

The doctor poked her head up over the drapes covering my knees. "Lovita, it's time to meet your baby. C'mon, give it all you've got!"

At the mention I mustered every bit of strength I had and pushed. And then—silence. My head fell back against the pillow as my breath left me. Though exhausted, I craned my neck to listen.

"Hudson? Hudson? I don't hear our baby. Is something wrong? Why don't I hear her crying?" My heart thumped fear.

Dr. Reed answered. "Hold on a minute, Lovita. Your husband is cutting the cord."

And then, I heard the most beautiful sound in the world. A little tiny voice began to cry and cry, and my heart melted. The nurse set our little one across my shoulder, her tiny perfect head against my neck. I promptly kissed her head and found Hudson's lips as he leaned in toward me.

Tears in his eyes, he reached out for her hand and she wrapped her teeny fingers around his pinkie finger. "We did it, Lovita. We have a beautiful baby girl."

Sue Jan called out from the other side of the room. "What did you all finally decide to call her? You've been so secretive the whole nine months."

I caressed her soft cheek. "Bess."

Hudson explained. "The name comes from Elisheba. In Greek it means, 'oath of God' or 'God is satisfaction.' but we're calling her Bess in memory of my mother, Bessie Mae Horton."

"Ita, that's a beautiful name, sweet and perfect. Your mama would love that you named your child after her, sort of. I'm glad you shortened her name to Bess instead of Bessie. I loved your mom, but naming your baby Bessie Mae would be asking a lot. So what's her widdle-middle name gonna be?" This time the voice was closer. "I've got to see that nugget." Suddenly, Sue Jan loomed over us, a big wide grin on her face.

"Bess Wynifred Hudson."

Sue Jan dabbed at her eyes. "Win a what?"

"Wynifred—Hudson's mama's name. She's from England."

Sue Jan's eyes might well have been spinning like those circus plates on poles, so I spelled it out for her. "Her name means 'windy village.'"

"A windy village, eh." She chuckled. "Do they eat a lot of beans in that there village? Hehe. Just saying. Foreign names are real different, aren't they? Twisting for Trystan? Win-a-Fred? Winnebago. No wonder you two kept the name to yourselves. And believe me, I'm not knocking your choice, but it would have been nice to get a few other options and opinions from people with better taste in choosing names. But even if your baby girl is named after a gassy village, Bess Win-a-Fred is darling. Presh! Adorbs! And she ain't no bigger than a cake of soap."

My hospital room had more flowers and stuffed animals and balloons than a flower shop, with visitors to match. It seemed like the whole town turned out to welcome baby Bess.

"I think her eyes are gonna be blue." Sue Jan stared intently at the baby in her arms. "Yup, blue."

Hudson stroked his chin. "I agree. From everything I've read up on, I think you're right." He touched my shoulder. "Are you comfortable, Lovita?"

"I sure am. When is your mother coming to see the baby?"

"Next week. And she's bringing my sister and aunt with her. You might not be able to hold the baby much while they're here. They're going to fall in love with our little Bess."

"That's okay. They might as well hold her as much as they can. It's too bad they live so far away."

A knock sounded on the door. "Come in," I said.

Sheriff Mel and the deputy joined us, hats respectfully at their chests. "She sure is pretty," Sheriff Mel cradled her head with his hand. "A little doll."

A nurse walked in to take the baby back to the nursery area for a while, and as she left I noticed the deputy holding a gigantic vase brimming with flowers. "They're so beautiful."

"Where can I put them?" he asked.

Hudson pointed to the shelves under the TV mounted on the wall. "Maybe on top of that? What do you think, Lovita?"

"Looks good to me. There isn't much room left in this place for flowers, or balloons or cuddle bears, or people," I laughed.

Crandall didn't waste any time. He plonked them down and took a seat.

Sheriff Mel smiled. "Lovita, you and Sue Jan did a great job of helping us track down suspects and rooting out answers. Me and Crandall want to thank you ladies for all the help you gave us in these investigations. Clint Greech was right about you two."

"We do love what we do," I said.

Sue Jan smirked. "We have to love what we do. If we didn't we'd be *loco en la cabeza.*"

"We thought we'd give you all an update on all the goings-on. I know you just had a baby and all, but would you like to hear?"

"Of course!" I nodded.

Sue Jan's eyes lit up. "And don't leave out any details."

The sheriff scratched the top of his head. "Let's see. I guess I'll start with Mordecai, Jr.. Sue Jan's nickname for him, 'the crazy clown psycho killer' really resonated with the newspaper and TV people. That's sort of what he's known by now. He confessed to killing Trystan because of his father's hatred for the man. His father blamed the family's misfortune on Trystan, because Mordecai Sr. lost the circus to him in a game of poker."

He cleared his throat. "Pickles was in the wrong place at the wrong time the day Trystan died. He witnessed the whole thing. Mordecai, Jr. also tried to kill off Johnny Roo and make it look like an accident because he believed Johnny helped Trystan cheat at the card game. His father suspected Johnny of spotting for Trystan, helping him cheat essentially. But he was unsuccessful in getting rid of him in the time he had, though he told us he intended to go back and finish the job later."

"Oh my goodness." Sue Jan put her hand over her mouth.

"Gerline confessed to poisoning Madame Curio for the insurance money. She made unsuccessful attempts at getting rid of Dixie as well. Dixie was the next person on Gerline's hit list."

"But Dixie is Max's sister." I said. "Didn't that bother her?"

His lips tightened together. "There's no evidence that it did."

"So Mordecai and Max and Dixie and Cornelia were sort of working together to try and take back the circus?" Sue Jan questioned.

"They were and they weren't according to Cornelia. She told me that she and Mordecai divorced when the kids were little, but the oldest son by his first marriage, Mordecai Jr. went to live with his father while the other two kids stayed with their mother. When the kids were grown, two plans were put into action by the two estranged parents, though neither was aware of the other's plans at first. Cornelia enlisted Dixie and Max to infiltrate the circus as performers and stage a financial takeover when the circus fell into ruin through a series of staged mishaps. But Max decided on his own to veer off their plan and romance Gerline to get in her good graces, though he wasn't sure at first if she'd even be interested in him. When Gerline did supposedly return his affections, he wound up falling in love with her. Dixie was upset about the relationship and told Max he was a traitor to their cause. She was really angry when she found out the two were engaged and told her mother all about it. Cornelia communicated threats to Gerline warning her to stay away from Max or something bad would happen. Cornelia made sure she was at your shop the day and time the circus was to arrive and caused a ruckus so everyone would remember she was there and stormed out. When the circus arrived, she doubled back and came in the back door of your salon, which I know for a fact you ladies usually forget to lock according to your husband, Sue Jan." He wiggled his finger at her. "She went up into the attic, set up her gun at the window and waited to take the shot."

"Did she tell you she was a circus sharpshooter when she was young?" I asked. "Sue Jan saw the circus poster with a picture of Cornelia on it."

"She told us all about it. Cornelia's real proud of being a sharpshooter, but she was also a trapeze artist. Taught her daughter."

"And on top of all those skills, she's kind of gross too." I added.

The sheriff's forehead creased up. "I—I recently became aware of that when we searched her apartment." He shook his head like he was trying to shake off the memory.

"Cornelia told me she didn't intend to hurt anyone, especially her own son, but the driver suddenly sped up which resulted in Max's injuries." Mel went on to explain that Gerline had sent the threatening notes to Zeke and Zara when Zeke started spilling the beans on some of the odd things happening at the circus attributing them to the circus curse. Gerline wanted to scare Zeke into keeping his mouth shut. But Zeke and Zara were also options on the insurance plan. The irony is that they were truly in danger, but from their boss, not a gypsy curse.

"I guess we didn't need that handwriting sample from Max then." Sue Jan rolled her eyes to the side. "It was a brilliant idea though, if I do say so myself."

"Well, there you have it." He threw up his hands. "Did I leave anything out? You all already know about Gerline's Bigfoot hoax. You saw Trick and Max at the cemetery. Trick was her hired henchman. He did all her dirty deeds, including the Bigfoot gig. Gerline did her homework on the creatures. She paid certain people to report bogus sightings to that Bigfoot research society. She even concocted a special Bigfoot scent to get the Bigfoot researchers hot on the trail looking for them."

Sue Jan crinkled her nose. "We still don't know why Trick and Max were three sheets to the wind."

"Trick has a drinking problem, remember?" I reminded her.

"But what about Max?" She asked. "Why was he wasted?"

Crandall answered. "Because he's heartbroke, that's why.

## WEIGHTY MATTERS

Gerline sent him in her place in the ring the last night of the performance knowing full well that Mordecai was gonna try and kill her. She was willing to let him die instead of her. I guess he realized that Gerline didn't love him the way he loved her."

Sue Jan pouted. "Poor guy. I know I shouldn't feel sorry for him, but I do."

Johnny Roo entered the room, knocking on the open door to be polite. "Yoo hoo? Could you stand one more visitor?"

"Johnny, thanks for coming." I said. "The nurse just took the baby back to the nursery for a while. You can see her through the viewing window if you like though."

"I would like that very much. As soon as I finish visiting with you, I'll go have a looksee." He sat in the only free chair near to the bed. "I have a few things I want to get off my chest to your girls." Johnny glanced at the sheriff. "And you all might as well know too. Mordecai Sr. thought I helped Trystan cheat at the card game that night. I'm insanely good at cards. I used to be a bit of a card shark when I was young. But I gave all that up. Trystan really helped me turn my life around for the better. He knew that Mordecai had some sort of grift going on and he asked me to even out the odds by spotting the card game and identifying how Mordecai was cheating. Trystan had a mic attached behind his ear. I had binoculars and a mic at my end. That's how Trystan won the card game. I told him exactly how Mordecai was cheating. To my way of thinking, Trystan won fair and square."

"Well, I'll be." I smiled at Sue Jan. "Crime doesn't pay."

"Mordecai, Jr. took revenge on an honest man, and all for nothing. His father was the one who cheated."

Sue Jan looked at Johnny. "Thanks for telling us that. Why didn't you speak up before?"

"Like I said to you that day we talked at the circus, I didn't trust you ladies at first. But when you offered to take care of me after back surgery, me a stranger, I knew you all were good people." He cleared his throat and directed his gaze at Sue Jan and Monroe. "And by the way, I won't be needing your help after all."

"Why not?" she asked.

"You got me to thinking about family and old times. Remember I told you I used to be in business with my brother? I hadn't talked to my brother in years. Well, I got in touch with him and he wants me to come back and be his business partner again. He promised to take care of me after the surgery too. So, I really appreciate your offer to help me out, but it feels good to know that I have a family to go home to."

"Johnny, that's wonderful." Sue Jan got up and gave him a big hug.

"Ouch!"

"Ugh, sorry." Sue Jan apologized. "I'll be glad when you get that back fixed."

"I oughta get going and leave you folks alone." He shook Hudson's hand. "Congratulations on your baby. Zeke and Zara are in the waiting room along with a whole bunch of other people. The nurses are having people come up and visit in groups so you don't have the whole town in here."

"One more question," I asked. "What's going to happen to the circus?"

He shook his head. "I expect it'll go belly up. Even with Gerline bringing in murder money, the circus was well on its way to bankruptcy." He shrugged. "Who knows? Maybe Max and Dixie and Cornelia will get their wish in the end and take over the circus again. That is, if they aren't behind bars."

"Minus Mordecai, for sure," Sheriff Mel added. "He'll be locked up for a very long time."

As soon as Johnny left, Pinkie Mountebank entered the room, removing his hillbilly hat as he did. He held a gigantic stuffed Sasquatch under one arm. "Thought I'd bring a little memento of meeting you fine people." He set it on the sofa and leaned over to have a look at the baby.

I smiled. "She's not here. Bess is in the nursery. You'll have to see her on your way out.."

"Well, I wanted to thank you all for helping out in the investigation. Too bad the Squatch turned out to be a hoax. Me and my team are understandably disappointed about not leaving with the proof we came here looking for, but that won't stop us from continuing to hunt down every clue and keep on searching for these creatures." He kissed my forehead and turned to go. "It's been a pleasure meeting you good folks." As he opened the door however, Pinkie turned on his heel. "Oh, and by the way, there's one thing I should mention. Those two fellers involved in the hoax don't tally up with all the sightings, and the casts of some footprints our team took don't match up with the costume footprints."

Silence engulfed the room.

"What are you saying?" Hudson asked.

"I'm a-saying that we can't offer a satisfactory explanation about some of the evidence we collected in the wooded areas around Wachita."

"You mean there might really be Bigfoots around here?" Sue Jan gulped.

Pinkie shrugged and smiled. "Without proof we can't be sure."

After Pinkie left, we had a big discussion about Sasquatches. Monroe showed up. And then Zeke and Zara. Jolene and Dr. Colley and Charla and her hunky camera man, "Mr. Wright." Tiff Purewhite and her teased web of hair showed up too. And our salon customers came to visit, and half the town, maybe more, before the nurses put a stop to all the visitors. At last, the only ones left in the hospital room besides me and Hudson were Sue Jan and Monroe. The nurse brought Bess back and placed her in my arms just as the sun started going down. Hudson opened the shades and we all stared out the window at breathtaking pinks and blues and oranges blending into a golden wash across the wide Texas sky.

Another nurse came in with a gigantic bouquet of beautiful yellow roses. "These just arrived." She placed them on a small side table next to my bed.

"Who are they from?" I asked.

She plucked the card out of the clear plastic trident securing it in the vase and handed the note to me.

As I began to read, my emotions got the better of me. Hudson, Sue Jan and Monroe were watching me, waiting for me to say something. "The roses. They're from Clint." I wiped my face with my bed sheet. "The note says, 'Lovita, you're like a daughter to me and I couldn't be prouder of you. You and Hudson take care. We'll be by to visit our 'grandbaby' as soon as we get back from our trip. With sincerest love and affection, Clint and Sandie Greech'."

I smiled up at my husband and let out a contented sigh. The events and emotions of the day had taken a toll on all of us. Hudson and Monroe decided to go down to the cafeteria to have dinner. Sue Jan promised to catch up with them as soon as the nurse brought my dinner. She scooted onto the edge of my bed and beamed at me.

"Suey, I've never been happier in my life."

"I told you there's nothing like being a mama." She jumped to her feet and twirled around. "Oh Mama-Ita, I'm so happy for you! I wish I could light up the night sky with fireworks and floodlights like they do in those fancy Hollywood movie premiers."

"You're such a nut. Shhh, you'll wake Bess," I cautioned.

Sue Jan cupped her hands around the sides of her mouth and whispered in the loudest 'whisper' I'd ever heard. "Send in the dancing lobsters! Lovita Mae Horton Taylor just had a beautiful baby girl!"

"Don't you mean, 'send in the clowns'?" I asked.

Sue Jan froze in the middle of another twirl and wagged a finger at me. "Never again, Ita. We're done with crazy red-nosed psycho clown killers. From now on, it's dancing lobsters. Got that?"

"Got it." I winked.

After Sue Jan left to join Monroe and Hudson in the cafeteria, I snuggled Bess and held her close, planting kiss after kiss on the little face still illuminated in the golden sunset. I began to hum ever so softly, the sweet songs and lullabies my mama used to sing to me. And somehow, some way, I knew my mama and daddy were singing right with me from heaven.

# NOTES & RECIPES

■■■■■■■■■■■■■■■■■■■■■■■■■

*From Sue Jan Pritchard Madson*
*Who Has Not Yet Confirmed Whether Or Not*
*She Will Be In The Running For Mayor In The Next*
*Mayoral Race in the Town of Wachita*

## Recipes For The Real Sasquatch Wives of Wachita

When I was thinking about recipes Sasquatches might find appealing, I found myself trying to get into them creatures' bison-sized heads. I realized that in order to figure out a Sasquatch, you gotta think like one. So I did. And I figured that if I was one of these big hairy-toe'd gals, I figure I'd appreciate a good natural-type cereal in case I was watching my figure. This recipe's got all kinds of grains and nuts and fruits that a creature like this might could gather in the woods, but the best part about the recipe is, there's a little touch of chocolate in the mix too. And women, whether they're nine feet tall and in need of a full-body waxing, or just a regular-size gal like myself in need of a minor upper lip wax from time to time, all appreciate something healthy with a little chocolate in it. Here's to you, Sassy Sister Sasquatch! You're welcome.

# Sasquatch Cereal

1-cup whole grain flakes
1 cup rolled oats
½ cup toasted wheat germ
¼ cup oat bran
2/3 cup chopped dates
½ cup dried figs, chopped
¼ cup dried apricots
¼ cup dried banana chips

1 Tbsp. sunflower seeds
1 Tbsp. pumpkin seeds
1 Tbsp. sesame seeds
1 cup mixed nuts (pecan, cashew, slivered almonds)
Chunks of chocolate
1 Tbsp. brown sugar
1 Tbsp. cinnamon or ground ginger

Preheat oven to 350 degrees.

Mix the grain flakes, oats and bran. (Then strap on your feedbag. Just kidding. Sounds like a great meal for a horse, doesn't it? But I promise you, this cereal is good for you and it tastes good too!) Spread the grain on a baking sheet with a rim so the cereal doesn't go all over your oven. Bake for 8 minutes until the grain mixture looks lightly toasted, (the way I like my marshmallows roasted), when you stir them with a spoon. Let cool, then dump out the mixture into a large bowl.

Stir in the seeds, dried fruits, nuts, and chocolate chunks, and spice. Transfer the muesli into an airtight container and store at room temperature for a couple of weeks.

*Personally I love squirrels and would never eat one of them cute little critters, even though technically, they're nothing more than limb rats. You know, rats that developed furry tails instead of those ugly rope-like nasty tails regular rats have. But some folks, like my cousin DeWayne and family, enjoy sitting down to a tasty Sunday Squirrel Supper on a regular basis. And folks like that will appreciate this recipe. I also believe that Sasquatch's would appreciate this recipe as well. Well, they would if they took the time to build a fire and cook. But I guess they mostly eat on the run, literally, on the run.*

## Squirrel Sauce Piquant

2 squirrels
3 medium onions, chopped
½ cup medium chopped green pepper
1 Tbsp. flour
1 can tomato sauce
Water
Cooking oil
Black pepper, red pepper, salt

Rub squirrels with salt, black and red pepper. Put oil in heavy iron pot ¼ inch deep. Brown squirrels on all sides and remove from pot. Lower fire to medium heat and sauté onions, green pepper and flour in remaining oil until brown. Place squirrels back in pot; add enough water to cover meat. Add tomato sauce. Cover and simmer on low fire 1-1/2 hours until tender.

*The words Sasquatch and Squash go together like beans 'n rice. Sorta like me and my BFF Lovita! So I knew this recipe had to happen. Plus, it's one of my personal faves. Squash casserole is the yummiest. My kids Marshal and Emma love this dish, and I'm sure Lovita's Baby Bess will soon be sitting in his high chair smearing it all over her head and face. I can't wait to go on Mommy Field Trips with Lovita. And I'm going to prove Zeke wrong about that Anti-gravity Room thing. Look out NASA, here we come!*

## Sa*squash* Casserole

1 lb. fresh squash
1 cup chopped shallots
¼ cup fresh mushrooms
½ cup quick oats
1 egg, beaten
Salt and pepper to taste

1 Tsp. salt
½ cup chopped celery
¼ cup pimento
¾ cup milk
2 hard-boiled eggs, chopped
Ritz crackers, crumbled

Cover squash with water, cook until tender. Drain and set aside. Sauté celery, shallots, mushrooms and pimento. Add to squash. Add remaining ingredients, except cracker crumbs, and place mixture in a buttered casserole dish. Bake at 400 degrees for 15 minutes. Remove from oven, cover with Ritz cracker crumbs and bake an additional 15 minutes.

ENJOY THE ENTIRE
# WHEN THE FAT LADIES SING COZY MYSTERY SERIES

### NOW AVAILABLE ON AUDIBLE!

*Misfortune Cookies*
*A Tisket, A Casket*
*Dead As A Doornail*
*That Wasn't Chicken*
*Felony Fruitcake*
*Weighty Matters*
*Custard's Last Stand*

### LISTEN TO ME ON THE RADIO!

I'M A HOST ON "ALONG CAME A WRITER" ON THE RED RIVER NETWORK, ON BLOGTALK RADIO!

# ABOUT THE AUTHOR

**Linda Kozar** writes both fiction and nonfiction titles, but is known for her cozy mysteries. She's a member of the American Christian Fiction Writers and was presented with their Mentor of the Year award in 2007, Advanced Writers and Speakers Association (AWSA), ChiLibris, Romance Writers of America (RWA), and Christian Authors Network (CAN), serving on the board as well. She also hosts the Along Came A Writer Radio Show on the Red River Writers network on BlogTalk Radio. She and Michael, her husband of 27 years, live in The Woodlands, Texas, and enjoy spending time with their two grown daughters, a wonderful son-in-law and Gypsy, their Jack Russell Terrier.

# FIND LINDA ONLINE

- **Linda's Website:** http://www.lindakozar.com
- **Gate Beautiful Radio Show:** http://www.blogtalkradio.com/search?q=gate-beautiful
- **Babes With A Beatitude Blog:** http://www.babeswithabeatitude.blogspot.com
- **Bookish Desires Blog:** http://bookishdesires.blogspot.com
- **Cozy Mystery Magazine Blog:** http://cozymysterymagazine.blogspot.com
- **Twitter:** https://twitter.com/LindaKozar
- **Facebook:** https://www.facebook.com/linda.kozar
- **Pinterest:** http://pinterest.com/lindakozar/boards/
- **Linked-in:** http://tinyurl.com/m8vspxu

Made in the USA
Charleston, SC
08 August 2016